# A Folly in Plotlands

## Dawn Knox

A Record of this Publication is available from the British Library.

ISBN: 9798399210230

This edition is published by An Affair of the Heart

Cover © Fully Booked

Editing – Wendy Ogilvie Editorial Services

To Mum and Dad.
Thank you for believing in me.

# Other books by Dawn Knox

# Chapter One

"Samira Stewart! Stop loitering!" Sister Mary Esme spoke with mock severity and smiled at the schoolgirl as she hesitated outside Mother Superior's office.

"Come on, dear, don't keep Sister Mary Benedicta waiting. You know she hates tardiness and procrastination ... you also know how much she hates your hair when you haven't tied it back," she added, fishing in her pocket for a piece of string and handing it to Samira.

"I'm sure you're not in trouble, dear, but it would probably help if you didn't look so guilty. Unless of course, you are guilty of something?" She smiled at the girl who was dragging her lustrous, black hair off her face into a ponytail and securing it with the string.

"That's the way," she said tucking a stray wisp behind Samira's ear and patting her shoulder. "Now, knock!"

Samira knocked.

At the sound of Mother Superior's deep voice instructing her to enter, she took a deep breath and opened the door.

There was nothing welcoming about Sister Mary Benedicta's office. It was cold and bare. The only item in the room that could be considered even slightly decorative was the simply framed painting of the Virgin Mary and infant Jesus which was hanging behind the desk.

There were no curtains, cushions or rugs and the fireplace had not been used for years. Sister Mary Benedicta did not approve of *fripperies* and *fol-de-rols;* terms she used to describe many of the things people commonly accepted as everyday comfort.

Samira hesitated at the door, staring at the two chairs in front of the desk. She'd been sent to the office many times during the last ten years to explain her behaviour but never before had she seen so much as a stool in front of the desk. Each time she'd been summoned to the study, she'd stood, weight shifting from foot to foot. Sweaty hands clasped behind her back as she squirmed with embarrassment and shame under the critical eye of Mother Superior while awaiting her punishment. But this time, there were two straight-backed wooden chairs opposite Sister Mary Benedicta.

"Ah, at last! Sit, please, Samira. I'm just finishing your documents."

All the other schoolgirls had been given a school report and character reference when their parents or guardians had arrived to pick them up from school. Despite there having been no word from Papa, the fact that her papers were being prepared, and the presence of the second chair, indicated he was coming. Samira felt torn. She was excited at the thought of seeing her father again after so long, but unhappy knowing her time at St. Theresa's Convent was finally over. She'd known this day would come eventually, but if she'd had word from her father announcing his arrival, she'd at least have had time to get used to the idea of leaving, rather than this very abrupt end to her school career.

She sat down on one of the uncomfortable chairs and watched with trepidation as Mother Superior's nib glided across the paper, leaving spidery, black loops in its wake. Samira felt like a pinned butterfly being scrutinised through a magnifying glass – except it wasn't her appearance that was being reviewed and judged, it was every one of her misdemeanours and failures during the previous ten years. If only she'd studied more ... behaved better ... tried harder. But it was too late now to influence what Sister Mary Benedicta was writing – the point of no return had been reached.

She consoled herself with the thought that if Papa took her home to India, she wouldn't be allowed to work, and therefore was unlikely to need either a school report or a character reference. But that merely underlined the uncertainty of her future.

*If Papa took her home?* Of course, he'd take her home! He wouldn't want his daughter to remain alone in a country at war. The sadness at realising her schooldays were over was followed by a rush of confusion and guilt.

How would Papa feel if, after not having seen his daughter for four years and after travelling halfway around the world to fetch her, she told him she wasn't sure she wanted to go back to India with him? Well, of course, he'd be desperately hurt. And who could blame him? But if, by some miracle, he permitted her to remain in England, would Sister Mary Benedicta allow her to stay and help the nuns? Samira had hardly been a star pupil, as Papa would no doubt shortly see from her report. Not that she'd been deliberately naughty – far from it, but the first seven years of her life had been spent in India and her memories were full of colour, excitement and mystery. So different from the grey, drab, monotony of life in the convent. It had taken the seven-year-old girl a long time to adjust. After all, coming from a household where servants were on hand to pamper and play with their master's children, and to carry out their every whim, the austerity of the convent had been a challenge.

For a while, it had seemed as though she would never belong in this whispering world of chanting and prayers. Her heart longed to fly in the warmth, noise and exoticism of India, but after ten years in the convent, she now wondered how she'd fit into the place of her childhood – especially since her mother had died.

When Samira had arrived at the convent at the age of seven, her memories of India had been frozen in time. Each night in the dormitory, she'd wept silently, consoling herself by re-living scenes from her past when she was still with her younger brother Vikash, Mama and Papa, as well as Mama's parents, Nana and Nani, on their tea plantation. She recalled the smell of spices hanging in the air, vases of vibrant flowers filling the house with their scent and colour, Cook feeding her delicious sweets ...

Her childhood had been perfect until she'd been sent to St. Theresa's Convent. Once in the heart of the Kentish countryside, she'd been expected to live a life as far removed from anything she'd previously known as if she'd been sent to the moon.

Samira first returned to India six years later, when Mama had become ill. It hadn't occurred to her anything would have changed, and she was shocked to find life was very different when viewed through the eyes of a thirteen-year-old. Papa had stayed by Mama's bedside and had sent a trusted family servant to England to collect Samira from school and accompany her home. By the time they'd reached the tea plantation in north-eastern India, Mama had already died and as custom decreed, the cremation had taken place the day after she'd died. Samira had been distraught at not having seen her mother to say goodbye, nor to have attended the funeral. Vikash had been at school in Calcutta, so he'd been at home for their mother's final few days and had kissed her before she passed away.

When Samira had finally arrived, Vikash had greeted her coldly. He'd pompously told her it was better she hadn't been there because she would have found it too upsetting and would probably have disgraced herself and the family by crying.

He'd described how the illness had apparently changed their mother from the beautiful, slender woman Samira held in her memory, to a wasted figure who looked lost in their parents' enormous bed.

Samira had been stunned at the change in her brother. At five years old, he'd been a loving, gentle boy, but eleven-year-old Vikash was turning into a young man without sympathy or warmth.

*Upset?* Of course, she'd have been upset. Of course, she'd have cried. She was devastated. But Vikash had inferred that whereas his sadness was noble, hers was somehow inferior. She noticed Vikash's attitude towards girls and women – his sister included – had altered, and now seemed to border on contempt. This change in the boy she remembered carrying on her shoulders and teaching to swim in the river – along with the pain of losing her mother – had increased her isolation. It caused her to question her place in the family. For the first time, she realised what she'd previously thought of as home – and yearned for while she'd been at St. Theresa's – was now alien to her. She found the Indian heat oppressive, the colours too bright, the smells too potent, and the crowded streets of the city overwhelming after the peace and calm of the convent.

But what had really disturbed her was the angry conversation she'd overheard between Papa, and Mama's brother, Uncle Rahul. It had given her nightmares that had only subsided once she'd arrived back in England and found sanctuary in the convent.

Until she'd left India at the age of seven, she'd never been aware that having an English father and an Indian mother was unusual. Her parents had been so in love and Mama's parents had accepted Papa and treated him as one of their own. He'd overseen the family's tea plantation and in his usual modest manner, he'd significantly improved and expanded the business.

Uncle Rahul had not been interested in growing tea and he'd spent much of his time in Calcutta where he'd married a wealthy heiress. When Mama's parents died, Uncle Rahul was happy for Papa to continue managing the family estates and he'd rarely visited – until Mama had died. There was something about Uncle Rahul that made Samira wary. She didn't know why because he was polite to her but the conversation she overheard that day confirmed her perceptiveness.

"She's old enough to marry." Samira heard him tell Papa.

"She's thirteen! I won't allow her to marry yet."

"You've lived here for years. You know our customs. She's old enough. I've started negotiations with a wealthy family—"

"You've what? How dare you! She's my daughter and I won't have her married off to someone to suit you or anyone else! She'll choose her own husband … when the time's right. And it's not right yet. Neither will it be, for many years."

"If you think I'll stand by and allow her to bring shame on our family like my sister disgraced ours, you're very mistaken—"

"I think you've said enough, Rahul. Take care! Rani and I inherited the plantation from your parents. Now it belongs to me. If they'd been ashamed of our marriage, they'd have left everything to you. Perhaps living in a big city has changed your values but I won't stand for any interference with how I bring up my daughter."

"Ah, so now I see why you were so keen to send her to England. You wish to find her an English husband. You wish to lose her Indian heritage."

"You see nothing, Rahul! I adored my darling Rani and I treasure her daughter's Indian heritage. I sent Samira to England to get a good education – nothing more. And when she's finished at school, then she will decide what she wants to do."

"Women do not decide—"

"Well, in my house, they do!"

Uncle Rahul had stormed off and Samira had run outside and hidden amongst the trees by the river, trying to make sense of the overheard conversation. The exchange between the brothers-in-law had barely lasted a minute, but it had shaken Samira to the core. Her uncle's words repeated over and over in her mind. How could Mama possibly have brought shame on the family because she'd married Papa? They'd been so in love. And how could Uncle think Samira would bring shame on her family unless she married someone of his choosing?

Marry?

At thirteen?

It was unbelievable. And yet, she knew girls did marry young in this part of the world. But she didn't feel she belonged to this society, nor that she had to obey its rules. Suddenly, she'd longed to return to England, to the safety and predictability of the convent ... and yet, she couldn't truly say she was happy there either, it was merely a refuge.

She simply didn't belong anywhere.

Once back at St. Theresa's, she'd settled into the routine, avoiding thoughts of the future, concentrating on her studies, and living in the moment. She still had another year at school before she needed to consider what she was going to do with her life – or so she thought. When war was declared, suddenly, everything changed.

"It's like the Great War, all over again," Sister Mary Martha had wailed in an unguarded moment.

"Thank you, Sister," Mother Superior had remarked sharply. "We don't need any hysteria in our convent."

"Sorry, Sister Mary Benedicta," the nun mumbled but Samira had seen tears well up in her eyes before she turned away. And it hadn't just been Sister Mary Martha who remembered the horrors of the war which had ravaged the world between 1914 and 1918. The older nuns seemed preoccupied, and although they were mainly silent, there was now a cloud of despondency hanging over the convent which was obvious to Samira and her fellow pupils.

The younger nuns had succumbed to the gloom; the singing from the chapel seemed to have acquired an added depth of emotion as if collectively, the sisters were taking it upon themselves to plead for the lives and souls of the whole world.

Ostensibly, nothing had changed. The nuns' routine carried on in the same way as it had since the order had been established, but the war had somehow penetrated the thick, stone walls of the convent and had swept away their peace.

Eventually, Sister Mary Benedicta who steadfastly resisted any change the world might try to impose on the order, had given in and had decided her sisters would be of more use nursing wounded soldiers than educating young girls, and she'd written to all the parents to tell them of her decision. One by one, the girls had left after tearful goodbyes in the dormitories and promises to keep in touch.

As soon as most of them had gone, lessons were discontinued. Samira and the other girls who were waiting for parents to come from far-flung places helped the nuns to carry medical supplies into the convent, clean and tidy the dormitories and make everything ready for the first influx of soldiers.

Gradually, parents arrived from glamorous locations such as Hong Kong, Canada, Australia – and took their daughters away, leaving Samira behind. Before the girls had departed, they'd talked about going home with varying degrees of enthusiasm but at least they were clear where their homes were. Samira envied them all.

With a flourish, Sister Mary Benedicta signed the final sheet, bringing Samira's thoughts back to the present. She blotted the page and folding the report and reference, she inserted them into a large envelope and looked expectantly at Samira.

"So, Samira, do you know what the future holds for you?"

"No, Sister Mary Benedicta, but I was wondering if it would be possible to stay ..."

"No, my child, that will not be possible. Very soon, we will have lots of men arriving. This is no place for a young girl. Unless of course, you intend to join our order."

"Oh no!" The words were out before Samira had time to consider. "I ... I mean I don't think I'm cut out to be a nun. I ... I just thought I might help with the nursing."

"That's not possible I'm afraid. You are not qualified and none of my sisters will have time to supervise you. The patients' welfare must come first. And surely, your family will have something planned for you? But a word of advice, Samira; you need to apply a little more thought to your life, think before you speak, and curb that hot-headed wilfulness you so often display—"

A knock at the door interrupted what was likely to become a lecture about Samira's faults.

"Come!" Mother Superior called.

Sister Mary Esme opened the door. "Mr Stewart here to see you, Sister Mary Benedicta." She smiled encouragingly at Samira.

"Show him in please."

The nun opened the door fully and Samira gasped, her hand flying to her mouth as if to stifle a scream. She knew her father had suffered bouts of malaria in the past, but he'd aged so much she hardly knew him.

If it hadn't been for the eyes, she might have passed him in the street without recognising him. His hair was thinner and very grey at the temples. He'd put on weight, especially around his middle and he seemed shorter. But his face! It was so familiar and yet so unknown. So *old*.

"Good afternoon, Mr Stewart," Sister Mary Benedicta said, rising and extending her hand to the visitor. "May I introduce you to Samira, your granddaughter."

# Chapter Two

**M**r Stewart started the ignition and turned the wipers on to clear the fine drizzle from the windscreen.

"Please wait!" Samira turned to gaze at the convent doors.

"Have you forgotten something, love?"

"No, it's just that ... I hoped Sister Mary Esme ..."

Gentle and loving Sister Mary Esme had been Samira's favourite. The other nuns were remote and disengaged from everything as if their bodies were still on earth, but their minds were already in heaven. It was Sister Mary Esme alone who'd made certain she'd been at the convent's enormous wooden doors to wave goodbye to each of the girls as they'd left school for the last time escorted by their parents or guardians.

Occasionally, one or two of the nuns who'd taught the girls had waited at the entrance with her, but bidding farewell to their pupils was obviously only a priority for Sister Mary Esme.

A tear trickled down Samira's cheek. She told herself all the nuns were busy preparing for the wounded soldiers and Sister Mary Esme would undoubtedly have been there if she could. Nevertheless, the pain of separation from everything familiar was somehow greater without the appearance of her favourite nun at the door to wish her

Godspeed. It felt as though she'd been forgotten already – and she hadn't even got as far as the convent gates.

Mr Stewart handed her a folded handkerchief and she wiped her eyes. "Is there anything I can do to make it better?" he asked.

She shook her head and dabbed at her eyes again. The handkerchief smelt of pipe tobacco, leather and spicy cologne. Strange, unfamiliar male odours.

"Is that her?" he asked.

Samira looked up and through her tears, she saw Sister Mary Esme with an apron over her habit and her sleeves rolled to her elbows, waving at the door. She'd obviously been in the middle of something but had taken the time to bid Samira goodbye. Fresh tears came to Samira's eyes, and she rolled down the window, leant out and waved back. The pain of separation was still there but at least now she knew she hadn't been forgotten.

"All right to go now?" Mr Stewart's voice was gentle.

"Yes, thank you ..." She'd paused, not sure how to address him. *Mr Stewart* sounded rather formal. She'd called her maternal grandfather *Nana* and grandmother *Nani,* much to the amusement of her friends at school, who'd pointed out that in England, *Nana* was another name for grandmother. She didn't think this man would want to be *Nana,* and anyway, the name belonged to her Indian grandfather.

Should she call him Grandfather? Grandpa?

He picked up on her hesitance. "So," he said jovially. "I imagine you're wondering what to call me? It must be strange to suddenly meet your grandfather after all these years."

She nodded.

"Do you have any suggestions?" he asked.

"What would you like me to call you?"

"Well, my daughter, Amelia's children call me Pop … that is, they used to when they were younger … I don't see much of them now." He sighed.

"Pop would be fine. And do I have a grandmother?"

"Yes, I'm taking you to see her now."

"What do you think she'd like to be called?"

"Um … oh … probably best you ask her," he said vaguely. "She can be a bit … well … a bit particular. Anyway, I expect you'll find that out for yourself soon enough. Now, you're not to worry about your father. He's much better and the hospital sent him home a few days ago, but it did mean he didn't know about your school closing. As soon as he found out, he sent me a telegram and asked me to pick you up."

"But why didn't anyone tell me he was in hospital? Are you sure he's all right now?" Samira bitterly regretted her earlier longing to stay in England. She now knew her place was in India, taking care of Papa.

"Yes, he's absolutely fine. He didn't go into detail about his illness, but he's fully recovered."

"How soon will I be able to leave?"

"Leave?"

"For India, to see Papa."

"Oh no, I'm sorry, love, you won't be leaving. Your father was quite insistent about that. He thinks it's too dangerous to travel by ship now we're at war."

"But if I don't go back to India, where will I go?"

"Well … yes … your father asked if I'd be able to look after you, but my cottage is rather small and … well …" He struggled for words. "Anyway, we … that is I … thought it might be best if you stayed with my niece, Joanna, and her family in Essex. She said she'd love to have you and you'll be better off in the countryside, rather than with … err – what with the war on. Anyway, it'll give you a chance to think about what you want to do with your life and as soon as the war's over, you can go home or do what you like."

If it hadn't been for the similarity she'd spotted between Pop's eyes and her father's, she might have wondered whether he was indeed her grandfather or an imposter. He seemed vague at times and almost embarrassed at others as if he was hiding something.

For a few miles, they drove through the Kent countryside in awkward silence which was finally broken by Pop.

"So, love, why don't you tell me about yourself? We've got loads to catch up on."

Samira told him about her life in India on the tea plantation in the lowlands of Assam in the Brahmaputra River Valley. She described the family's white bungalow with its covered verandas. The backdrop of lush vegetation covered in vibrant flowers which filled the house with perfume. And nearby were the fields of tea bushes, where women in colourful saris and large baskets on their backs picked leaves with amazing speed and dexterity. She spoke of St. Theresa's Convent, her school friends, and the nuns, and made him laugh with her impression of Sister Mary Benedicta denouncing the world's fondness for *fripperies* and *fol-de-rols*.

But she didn't tell him how lost she was – how she was torn between two worlds – because that was the sort of thing that you confided in someone special, and this man who she'd just met was still a stranger. And worse, he was a stranger with a secret who she couldn't bring herself to trust. He was obviously in touch with Papa, so why hadn't he known about her past? Or perhaps he did, and he just wanted to get her to talk and put her at ease.

"Perhaps you'll tell me a little about your life, Pop," she said, hoping he'd reveal why he was being so vague.

"Well ..." he began, and Samira noted yet more hesitation. "Well ... there's not much to tell – nothing to interest you really. I live in a small village in Sussex called Ribbenthorpe, and I own a hardware store in town. All very dull."

There was so much she wanted to know. Why hadn't he seen Auntie Amelia's children – her cousins – for some time? Why didn't he appear to know much about her and Vikash? She didn't remember her father ever having mentioned him or her grandmother. Perhaps there'd been a family row and Pop didn't want to admit it.

Fields and meadows had given way to suburban sprawl and leafy avenues, then to streets of terraced houses with iron railings. Mothers pushed prams along the busy streets with children of varying sizes hanging on to their skirts, and dogs wandered, dodging between the cars and buses. She was sure Pop had said he was taking her to see her grandmother, but this didn't look like a sleepy Sussex village.

"Where are we?" she asked in alarm.

"We'll be crossing over the river on the Woolwich ferry soon. Look, you can just see the Thames."

The Thames. They were already in London. Samira was disappointed. Pop seemed to have forgotten he'd said he was going to take her to see her grandmother. Instead, they were obviously going straight to Essex, to his niece's house. Perhaps he was tired. It had been a long drive and she was almost nodding off. Perhaps, she'd meet her grandmother another day.

But once they'd crossed the river, instead of going east towards Essex, Pop turned west, towards central London.

Shops and pubs lined the busy streets jostling for a place between churches and narrow alleys and as they drove through the increasing traffic she spotted market stalls, a cinema, several synagogues, countless factories and even a bell foundry. Samira was just about to ask where they were when Pop turned left off the main road.

"Not much further," he said, "but before you meet Ivy ... er, your grandmother, I think I need to explain something. I've been wondering how to break this to you for most of the journey but there's no easy way to say it ... and you need an explanation. So, I'm just going to come out with it. Please don't be too hard on me. You don't know me yet and I would like that to change, really, I would, but things are very complicated. And you may decide you're better off without me in your life."

He pulled up in Aylward Street and turned the engine off although he made no attempt to get out of the car.

"It's like this, Samira. Your grandmother and I don't really get on. We haven't done for years. I expect you'll see for yourself; she can be a difficult woman and probably more so because I didn't have time to let her know we were coming. Ivy and I haven't lived together for a long time. I still pay for her to live in our house, but I moved out into a cottage in Sussex. She's never forgiven me, of course ... and ... well, I suppose I'd better tell you the whole truth because if I don't, Ivy probably will ... I met someone else in Sussex and well ... we live together. Now I know you're probably shocked. I'm not proud of it and my two children – David, your father, and your Auntie Amelia – were pretty angry with me, which is one of the reasons I don't see much of them – or my grandchildren ... Although, I'm going to mend those rifts in time." He paused and gripped the steering wheel tighter, then sighed.

"But the other reason is that my ... er lady friend, Edie ... and I have two children of our own. So, not only have you acquired grandparents today, but you also have two aunties who are only a few years younger than you." He paused and looked at her pleadingly, "Please don't judge me too harshly until you've met Ivy. She can be quite a handful but please don't think I'm trying to shift the blame. Marriage should be for life, and I've broken my marriage vows ... Say something. Please. Even if it's that you think I'm a disgrace and you're ashamed of me ..."

The confession had shocked Samira, but it was hard to be emotional about people she hadn't known existed until a few hours before. She imagined it must have been much harder for Papa and Auntie Amelia – and of course, for her grandmother.

"Well, we'd best get it over with," he said with a sigh, misinterpreting her silence for condemnation. "At least I had a lovely journey getting to know you before you knew about me. At least I had that."

She placed her hand on his arm and when she saw the glimmer of hope in his eyes, she smiled.

"Mama always said you should never condemn or criticise anyone until you've walked a mile in their footsteps."

He laid his hand on hers and with tears in his eyes, he said, "Your mama was a very wise woman and I wish with all my heart, I'd met her."

There was a tap on the car window and a stout woman with her hair in rollers covered by a scarf crossed her beefy arms and glared at them.

Pop rolled the window down. "Good afternoon, Mrs Thomsett. How are you and your family?"

"All fine and dandy, thank you, Mr Stewart. Come to visit Mrs Stewart, 'ave yer?" She bent down to get a better look at Samira and glared at her.

"Yes, I've brought my granddaughter, Samira, to see Ivy—"

"Oh! Granddaughter! I thought she might be yer fancy woman. Oh yes," she said screwing up her eyes to get a better look at Samira. "You must be Davy's daughter. I can see you've got a touch of the exotic about you. Welcome, lovey, welcome. Although prepare yerselves. Ivy ain't at 'er best."

"Is she ever?" Pop's shoulders sagged.

Mrs Thomsett's expression changed. She looked over her shoulder at number 10, as if she expected someone to be watching, "No, Mr Stewart, I mean *really* not at 'er best. We had to call Dr Jenkins in yesterday after she had a turn. But I would think 'er granddaughter would be just the tonic she needs."

"Thank you, Mrs Thomsett, I really appreciate your help." He tried to slip some money into her hand, but she stepped back, refusing to take it.

"Ain't no need," she said, shaking her head.

"There are bound to be expenses and it's not fair you should have to pay, Mrs Thomsett. It's so good of you to keep an eye on Ivy. We both know she can be a challenge. Please take this ... for the children, perhaps."

"Well, that's very kind of you, Mr Stewart," she said taking the pound note and tucking it into the enormous pocket of her apron. "I've put the key back under the front mat as usual. Right, I'll leave you to it ... Cheerio," she added. She stooped to pick a toddler up from the pavement, settled him on her hip and strode towards two young boys who were circling each other with fists raised. She warned one of them what his mother would do when she found out, grabbed the other by the ear and marched him back to number 12.

"Mrs Thomsett has a heart of gold," said Pop. "She calls a spade a spade, as you may have noticed. But I like that. At least you know where you stand with her. It's when people talk behind your back things get unpleasant." He sighed as if he'd been the subject of a great deal of gossip. "Well, it's no point putting it off any longer, come and meet your grandmother."

# Chapter Three

The commotion had been enough to bring Mrs Thomsett rushing back into number 10, from next door.

"Ooh, not that lovely china milk jug." She stooped to pick up the broken pieces. "Now, Mrs Stewart, you look like you're getting yourself in a right ol' state. Why don't I put the kettle on, and we'll all have a nice cuppa? What d'you say?"

"I'm not drinking anything while that man is in my house." The woman's voice was cold. She pointed a finger at her husband who stood protectively in front of Samira.

Pop had led Samira into the kitchen where his wife had been dozing in an armchair next to the fire, wrapped in a tartan blanket. When she realised who her visitor was, she'd picked up the nearest object and hurled it.

"You've got no right to be here. Get out!" She seized her empty cup.

"Now, now, Mrs Stewart." Mrs Thomsett's tones were coaxing and gentle as if speaking to a child. "Why don't you put that down. It's part of your best china set. You wouldn't want it broken, would you? Mr Stewart has brought your granddaughter to meet you. What d'you think of that?"

"Granddaughter?" The woman tried to stand but the effort was too much, and she sank back into the chair. "Don't be ridiculous, woman, I don't have any grandchildren."

She pointed at Pop. "You! Get out! You've got no right creeping in here as if you own the place!"

Ignoring the fact that he did own the place, he tried a gentle approach. "Ivy, I know you're angry with me. You've got every right to be, but there's something you need to know—"

She held up her hand. "I don't have to listen to anything you say. Now get out. Can't you see the nurse has come to see to me? Get out! And don't come back!"

Silence.

Eyes swivelled left and right, searching for the nurse the woman had referred to.

"Blimey, it's worse than I thought," whispered Mrs Thomsett. "I knew she were bad, but I didn't know she were seeing things. Shall I telephone the doctor?"

"I … I don't know," said Pop uncertainly.

"Nurse! If you take my advice, you'll move away from that man. He is *not* to be trusted," she said looking straight at Samira who was peeping out, wide-eyed, from behind Pop.

"Blimey, she thinks you're a nurse, lovey," Mrs Thomsett whispered. "It must be the school uniform."

It occurred to Samira that for the first time in her life, she was involved in a situation where the adults had no idea what to do and that she was the only one who could offer a solution. She smoothed her navy-blue gymslip with perspiring hands, patted her hair to ensure it was tidy, and stepped forward. It had been fortunate Sister Mary Esme had reminded her to tie her long hair back into a ponytail, as she doubted nurses would be allowed to have their hair loose.

"Mrs Stewart," she said, offering her hand. "My name is Samira, and I am very pleased to meet you. Perhaps you would permit me to make you a fresh pot of tea." She prayed her grandmother would not require anything more complicated, personal or medical, than that.

"At last! Someone with manners! Yes, please, nurse, I would like some tea and perhaps you'd be good enough to show *him* out. He's upset me enough for one day." Her hand shook, as she pointed an accusatory finger at Pop.

"Perhaps, Mr Stewart," Samira said, her eyes pleading with Pop. "It might be best if you leave. I'll show you out ..."

Mrs Thomsett followed Pop and Samira into the hall.

"Well, it looks like it's under control, so I'll leave you to it. You're a good girl," she said patting Samira's shoulder.

"I'll go to the Post Office on the corner and telephone Joanna to find out what time she expects to arrive to pick you up. Will you be all right until I get back?" Pop asked.

"Yes, I think so. I'll just make tea and chat to ... to my grandmother for a while."

"I won't come in the house again – it upsets her too much, so I'll send Mrs Thomsett or one of her family in with a message."

Samira hurried back to her grandmother in the kitchen, tucked the blanket around her and placed the kettle on the range next to the fire.

"Thank you, nurse. Well, it's certainly good to know Dr Jenkins is so thoughtful, although he didn't mention anything about sending you," the woman said. "But I'm very glad you're here. I don't like Mrs Thomsett dropping in without a by your leave. She's such a gossip and I don't like the whole neighbourhood knowing my business. Sometimes it's easier to deal with strangers, don't you think? It puts everything on a professional footing."

Samira busied herself making a fresh pot of tea, answering, "Oh yes, Mrs Stewart," and, "definitely," where appropriate.

She was beginning to have second thoughts about allowing her grandmother to believe she was a nurse. It was deceitful, but at least now, she was calm. And making someone tea and ensuring they were comfortable was hardly dishonest.

If only Mrs Thomsett or a member of her family would come in to let her know when Joanna would be arriving. Now Pop had gone, Grandmother seemed quite rational, even if she was rather weak. Samira wondered whether her claim that she didn't have any grand-children was due to confusion. After all, as far as Samira knew, she had three grandchildren besides herself and Vikash. Auntie Amelia had Hannah, Joseph and Jack. But perhaps what she'd meant was that she never saw them, rather than she didn't know they existed.

There was a gentle tap at the kitchen door and when Samira opened it, a small girl held out a note. "Me gran says I'm to give you this, miss." Samira thanked her and unfolding the paper, she read it.

"If you'll excuse me, Mrs Stewart, I won't be a moment." Samira walked towards the front door.

"Where are you going, nurse? You won't be long, will you?" Her gran's face had gone white, and she gripped the arms of the chair.

"No, no, I'll be right back."

"You're not just saying that, are you?" There was a note of panic in her voice.

"No, Mrs Stewart, I'll be a minute, that's all. I promise I'll come back."

How would her grandmother react when Joanna came to take Samira home?

Pop was waiting on the front doorstep. "Oh Samira, love, I've just spoken to Joanna's husband, Ben, on the telephone. He said her car's broken down in Ilford and he's going to drive there and pick her up. But that means Joanna won't be able to fetch you today. I'm afraid I'm going to have to find a room in a hotel for you tonight. I'd love to take you home, but I really can't. I know I said there wasn't enough room in our cottage, and that was true, but the real reason is that Edie – my lady friend – has a jealous streak and doesn't like any reminders that I'm married ... well ... anyway, it's just not possible, I'm afraid. I'm so sorry, love, I really am."

He looked so dejected; Samira felt sorry for him. His life appeared to be so complicated.

"Nurse! Nurse!" Her gran's voice could be heard rising in panic.

"She doesn't want me to go," said Samira. "What shall I do?"

"This is a disaster! I'm sorry, love, I had no idea she was so disorientated. I've never seen her like this before. She's usually prickly, but this is something new. Normally, she's suspicious of people, she barely tolerates Mrs Thomsett going into the house, but she certainly seems to have taken a shine to you. I'm afraid we're just going to have to leave Ivy to it. It's a shame but I need to find you somewhere to stay before I can go home."

He checked his watch and frowned. "Edie will already be at the window waiting for me, so I need to hurry."

"Nurse! Where are you?" The exasperation and fear could be heard in her gran's voice.

"Pop, I can't just walk out and leave her! It would be cruel. I told her I'd be back."

He bit his lower lip. "I don't think we've got much choice ..."

"Unless ..." said Samira, almost afraid to voice her suggestion.

"Yes?" Pop's eyes lit with hope.

"Unless I stay with her tonight. Perhaps in the morning, Mrs Thomsett could phone for the doctor to come, and he could have a word with her. And then Joanna could take me home tomorrow."

"Well, that would solve the problem." His eyes were full of hope. "But it's an awful lot to ask of you."

"It might give me a chance to get to know my grandmother a bit – even if she doesn't seem to know who I am."

"Ah, about that ... I'm afraid she may have spoken the truth about not knowing she had grandchildren."

Samira looked at him aghast. "How is that possible?"

"Because our son and daughter severed all ties with her and neither of them told her when the grandchildren were born. It's very sad but Ivy made their lives miserable. She tried to control them and ended up alienating them both. I thought one day she'd mellow – not towards me of course – but I always hoped she'd be reconciled with her children. I've tried to persuade them both, but so far, they won't hear of it. So, I'm pleased that even though she doesn't know you, she'll be able to spend time with you."

"Nurse!"

Pop brought Samira's suitcase and bag and put them in the hall. He took her hand and kissed it. "We're still strangers, so I won't kiss you on the cheek, but one day, I hope we'll really be granddaughter and grandfather."

He waved to her as he drove off down the street, several small children running beside him until he reached the corner and was gone.

Samira went back into her gran's kitchen.

"Ah, Nurse! You came back." Gran sank back into her chair, her bird-like hand splayed over her heaving chest.

"Yes, Mrs Stewart, I told you I would."

"That's what they all say. But sooner or later, everyone leaves." Her voice trailed off to a whisper. "It's just a fact of life."

# Chapter Four

S amira woke early the next morning, unaccustomed to the sounds in the street outside. The clip-clop of the horse's hoofs as it pulled the milkman's cart along the cobbled road and the rattle of the glass bottles of milk in metal crates, roused her.

It was still dark when she got out of bed and washed her face in the china bowl that stood on the tallboy in the corner of her bedroom. Despite sleeping in a strange bed, she felt refreshed, and anyway, she was used to rising early in the convent.

The previous evening her gran had been worn out after her angry outburst. She'd refused anything to eat and had announced she wanted to go straight to bed.

"You'll stay, won't you, nurse? There's a spare bedroom opposite mine. I might need you in the night."

Samira made her hot cocoa and Mrs Thomsett had popped in to help her up the stairs to bed. She'd expected to be called during the night, and had lain awake for some time, disturbed at the prospect of what her grandmother might need. But other than the occasional bout of snoring, Gran had been quiet.

When Mrs Thomsett arrived in the morning with a cheery "Coo-ee!", Samira had already laid the table and put the kettle on the range.

"I'll 'elp her down the stairs, lovey, and then I'll nip along to the Post Office and telephone Dr Jenkins. You're a little marvel!" she said smiling at Samira. "It's such a shame Mrs Stewart doesn't know who you are but there were harsh words spoken between her and your Pa. Young Davy were a lovely lad. I were quite upset when he left ... And then to find he'd gone all the way to *India!*"

She spoke as if India was on the outer reaches of the universe. "But Mrs Stewart would insist on threatening to cut Davy and his sister, Amelia, off ... sometimes, giving a child an ultimatum is the best way to lose them. 'Ark at me going on as if I'm an expert! I've got so many children and grandchildren; it might be an idea if I gave one or two of them an ultimatum and lost a few!" She laughed loudly.

The small girl who'd delivered the note the previous day poked her head around the kitchen door. "Nan, you'd better come quick, Sid and Georgie are fighting again."

"You tell them I'll 'ave their guts for garters if they haven't made up by the time I find them, Rosie. I'm just going to 'elp Mrs Stewart downstairs. Run along now. When I've finished, you can come to the Post Office with me."

Rosie nodded and skipped out.

"What's she doing in here again?" Gran asked Samira when Mrs Thomsett returned after her phone calls.

"I'm just seeing if your nurse wants anything, Mrs Stewart. Just being neighbourly."

"Huh! Snooping more like!"

"Oh no!" said Samira. "Mrs Thomsett has been really kind ..."

"Don't you worry, lovey, I don't take no notice," Mrs Thomsett whispered. "Dr Jenkins will try to call later and check her out, and Joanna will be here just after lunch. So, not much longer. D'you think you can bear it?"

"Oh yes! She's no trouble, at all—"

"What are you two whispering about?" Gran asked.

"Nothing, Mrs Stewart, I'm just telling yer nurse the best place to buy a loaf of bread." She winked at Samira and added loudly. "As I said, it's Patterson's Bakery around the corner."

When Mrs Thomsett had gone, Samira tried to make conversation, but she soon discovered her grandmother would neither talk about Pop nor her children. In desperation, she talked about her childhood in India and for the first time, Gran took an interest.

"I thought there was something foreign about you," she remarked. "But you're a pretty thing – and very kind too." It was as if she considered prettiness and kindness were qualities sufficient to make up for the regrettable foreignness.

"In fact." Her voice became wistful. "You remind me a bit of my son, Davy. Not that you look anything like him," she said quickly. "He had blonde curls when he was young and such a gentle manner …" She trailed off, her eyes narrowing as if remembering something unpleasant. She took hold of Samira's wrist and spoke urgently as if passing on vital information.

"Let me give you a word of advice, nurse. You're only young, so you may not have found this out for yourself yet, but you will, mark my words, you will. People may promise you the world, but in the end, they'll let you down. In the end, everyone leaves. Take every chance you get to be independent. It's not easy for a woman. The law's been against us for so long, not allowing us the vote until recently, not allowing us to take charge of our own destinies. But the war will change things. You mark my words. Things changed for women after the last war, and they'll change again. Put by as much money as you can, so when you're finally on your own, you'll be all right ..." She dabbed her eyes with a handkerchief.

If Samira could have thought of something to say, she wouldn't have been able to voice her feelings because of the lump in her throat. She felt so sorry for this woman – her grandmother – who seemed to drive away anyone who might care for her and then bear a grudge against them when they left.

A loud rat-a-tat-tat at the door brought them both back to reality and Samira rose to open the door. A smartly dressed young woman with chestnut curls framing a heart-shaped face stood on the doorstep. She smiled with relief when she saw Samira.

"I hoped you'd answer the door," she said holding out her hand. "I'm Joanna. Uncle John said Aunt Ivy was being even more difficult than usual and I know I'm not her favourite person ... Anyway, I'm so sorry about not picking you up yesterday but the car conked out on Ilford Broadway. You should have seen the traffic hold up. Anyway, I've got Ben's car today and that seems to be running smoothly, so as soon as you're ready, we'll head back to Essex. If you want to get your things together, I'll go and have a word with Aunt Ivy ... or more likely, she'll have a few insults to throw at me."

Samira was drawn to the young woman who was probably only ten years her senior. She seemed to be full of confidence, and the upturned corners of her mouth gave her face a permanently happy expression.

"Nurse! Who's at the door? What's going on?" shouted Gran from the kitchen.

Joanna blanched. "The last time I saw Aunt Ivy, I was only eighteen and she used to frighten me to death with her sharp tongue. Nine years later, I'm married with two children of my own and I still feel terrified. You deserve a medal for putting up with her last night."

"Nurse!"

"Right," said Joanna checking her hat in the hall mirror and taking a deep breath. "Let's get it over with."

Samira opened the kitchen door.

"Who is it, nurse?" Gran asked, her voice croaky from her earlier shouts.

"You've got a visitor, Mrs Stewart."

"A visitor? I never have visitors. Can't you get rid of them? I don't want to see anyone."

Before Joanna could step out of the gloom of the hall into the kitchen, the front door opened.

"Coo-ee! Only me. I've brought the doctor." It was Mrs Thomsett and a thin, bald man with a worried expression who hovered uncertainly in the doorway. He passed his leather briefcase from hand to hand.

"What is this? Paddington Station? What are all these people doing in my house? Get out! Nurse, show them all out!"

Dr Jenkins' professionalism took over and he glided past Mrs Thomsett and Joanna in the narrow hall.

"Now, Mrs Stewart, you really must calm down. Your heart isn't strong, and you need to rest."

"How can I rest with all these people in my house? Who is that woman in the hall?"

Joanna stepped into the kitchen.

"Aunt Ivy—"

"No!" she screeched, her hands gripping the arms of the chair and her face contorted with rage. "I thought I told you never to cross my threshold again—"

"Enough!" roared Dr Jenkins. "Ladies and ... *you*," he said to Samira. "Please leave. No one will come in again until I say so. Mrs Stewart needs peace and quiet."

"Please don't send the nurse away, doctor. She's been a godsend," Gran's voice trembled.

Dr Jenkins emerged from the house sometime later. He explained he'd given his patient something to calm her down and said she'd probably be sleepy for the rest of the day. He forbade Joanna to go back in the house and despite his misgivings at passing off a schoolgirl as a nurse, he had to admit, she had a calming effect on his patient. Reluctantly, he suggested Samira might stay for a few days.

"So, she will recover, then, doctor?" Joanna asked.

He shook his head sadly. "No. I'm afraid not. The damage to her heart is too great, and any agitation is extremely bad for her. To be honest, I'm amazed she's lasted this long. But she's a determined woman. Who knows, she might last for weeks."

"But Samira can't stay here for weeks. Perhaps Uncle John could find a live-in nurse."

"Well, good luck with that." Mrs Thomsett crossed her arms across her chest. The doctor nodded in agreement.

"Well, I could stay here ... for a while," Samira suggested timidly. "We were getting on well this morning. And it's not like I have any plans, so it might be the best thing for all of us. With the war on, I could make myself useful and do some voluntary work ..."

"Are you sure? It seems as if everyone wins except you, darling," Joanna said.

Samira nodded; her voice more confident. "Yes, I'm sure. If I can't cope, I'll let Mrs Thomsett know and perhaps she can contact you, Joanna. But so far, it hasn't been hard, and it will give me a chance to get to know the grandmother I never knew I had."

# Chapter Five

It was late September, but the breeze was wintry, and the heavy clouds raced across the sky, threatening rain. Samira shivered, did up the buttons on her uniform overcoat and straightened her hat. The night promised to be long, uncomfortable and dangerous.

Already this evening, several bombs had dropped on London, exploding far to the west. The sky now glowed red, and the wind carried a hint of oily smoke. Samira had joined the Women's Voluntary Service a few months before, so she had some idea of what those poor people on the other side of London must be going through. She wondered how the firefighters and members of the other organisations that had been set up to handle wartime disasters, were coping. One thing was certain – there would be chaos.

The Germans had increased their bombing raids over London, in what the newspapers were calling *The Blitz*. Luftwaffe pilots targeted industrial areas and the East London Docks, trying to cause maximum disruption. Their ferocious and sustained night-time aerial attacks were also devastating nearby Stepney and the other East London residential areas, killing large numbers of civilians and making thousands destitute.

Samira and the other WVS members had been increasingly busy, serving refreshments to dazed victims whose homes had been bombed, as well as to the men and women in the various rescue services.

When Gran had discovered Samira was expected to pay for her own WVS uniform, she'd insisted on accompanying her to Harrods and buying every item of clothing, despite making it clear she didn't approve of her being out at night. Samira had been touched at her generosity, and that evening, she was more grateful than ever to be wearing the grey-green tweed overcoat over her WVS suit.

Gran had recovered some of her strength and gradually, she'd stopped referring to Samira as a nurse. Had she remembered Mrs Thomsett mentioning she was her granddaughter? If Gran suspected Samira's true identity, she'd never mentioned it again – nor even hinted at it. Samira didn't see any point in raising the issue. No good could come from bringing everything out in the open. It took very little to agitate the elderly lady and that was bad for her health.

Gran treated Samira like a distant family member and live-in carer. And she now called her 'Samantha' because, in her opinion, it sounded less foreign than her given name. Samira had been relieved she hadn't insisted on the more formal *Miss Stewart,* raising the possibility of a discussion on their shared surname. Gran, who Samira addressed as *Mrs Stewart*, was still prickly and difficult, but it felt as though a relationship was developing between them, even if it was hard to define exactly what the bond was.

"Penny for 'em!" An attractive girl with shoulder-length auburn hair and a dusting of freckles across her nose came around the corner of the tea van and found Samira deep in thought. Kitty Fletcher, also dressed in a WVS uniform, was the unofficial leader of the girls and had taken Samira under her wing when she'd first joined several months before. It had been obvious there was a world of difference between the Cockney girls and the slim, dark-haired young woman who'd been born in India but had spent much of her life in a convent.

When Kitty first introduced Samira to the other girls, Mavis, one of the local girls, had asked her if she spoke English. The others had stared at her with suspicion. But with Kitty's determination that her team would work together, she set about finding similarities between the girls and ignoring differences. It had taken a few days but once the local girls realised Samira's English was better than theirs and that she was quick to learn and keen to exceed anyone's expectations, they accepted her as one of them.

Mavis had been impressed that Samira was taking driving lessons from Kitty. "I don't know how you do it," she said when she'd seen Samira at the wheel. "I wouldn't dare." Kitty had been pleased to teach Samira to drive the van – the more skills they shared, the more effective they'd be in their war effort.

"Why're you so deep in thought?" Kitty asked.

"Oh, I was just thinking about Mrs Stewart and hoping if the siren goes off, she'll go under the stairs. I know she doesn't like it under there."

Samira had been vague about her relationship with Gran, hinting she was a distant relative.

"Doesn't your neighbour keep an eye on her?"

"Yes, but she's such a handful and Mrs Thomsett's got family of her own to gather up and keep safe."

"You're doing the right thing, you know," said Kitty. "You could stay home and look after her or you could help lots of people who're really in need, with us."

"Yes, I know. I just feel so sorry for her. She looks so lost when I leave in the evening."

"Well, let's take your mind off it before the other girls arrive. We've time for a drive around the block if you'd like."

Before Samira could get to the driver's seat, the air raid warning siren began to wail; rising and falling. The din cut through the darkness. It didn't matter how many times she heard it; the sound still made the hairs on the back of her neck rise. People tumbled out of their houses, clutching flasks of tea, blankets, cushions and bags, heading for the public shelter.

"It's going to be lively tonight," said Kitty a little later, as the *ack-ack* of the anti-aircraft guns cut through the air, and bombs dropped to the east. "It looks like they're targeting the docks again."

Many of the fires caused by the incendiary bombs had been extinguished but there were sufficient flames to light up the dockland area showing the German pilots where to bomb. By the early hours, Samira was exhausted. She'd served tea to the air raid wardens and firefighters, as well as civilians. Many had been evacuated from dangerous buildings and some stood near the WVS van, comforting each other, or staring at the pile of rubble that had once been their homes. Many people had been wounded by falling masonry and Samira and the other girls had helped to dress minor wounds and lead people to safety.

"All right, miss? You look done in," a young air raid warden said to Samira. "I don't suppose there's any chance of a cuppa?" he added smiling cheekily.

He took off his tin helmet and wiped his forehead with his sleeve, smudging soot across his face.

"James McGuire," he said, holding out his hand. "But everyone calls me Jimmy."

"Samira Stewart." She shook his hand. "And yes, there's every chance of a cuppa."

But before she could go back to the van, screams ripped through the night followed by the rumble and crash of a building collapsing. Jimmy turned and sprinted away, joining the other air raid wardens who were running towards the source of the sound. In an instant, they were lost to sight amongst the smoke and dust.

It was almost light before the bombing ceased, and Kitty was satisfied the van was clean and tidy. The fires were out, although here and there, smoke billowed upwards into the grey dawn and the smell of charred wood filled their nostrils. She thanked the girls and told them to go home and get some rest if they could.

"Ain't that Mary McGuire's younger brother lurkin' over there?" asked Lizzie pushing her smeared spectacles further up her nose.

"Yeah, that's Jimmy," said Mavis. "He lives around the corner to me. It looks like he's eyeing up our Sam, don't it, ladies?"

The other girls laughed good-naturedly, and Samira blushed.

"I'm sure he's not," she muttered and turned away to hide her flaming cheeks.

As the other girls walked home in ones and twos, Samira set off for Aylward Street alone and Jimmy fell into step beside her.

"I hope you don't mind me waiting for you, but I wanted to apologise for rushing off like that and I ... I hoped perhaps we could still have a cup of tea together ... later. That is if you're not too busy. Or you're not seeing ... anyone else."

He reminded Samira of a puppy with expressive eyes that begged her not to turn him away.

"Well, I don't know ... it's just that my ... aunt ... isn't very keen on me going out."

"That's all right," he said, his face registering, first disappointment and then resignation. "I understand."

"No," she said quickly, reluctant to hurt his feelings. "It's not that I don't want to, it's just I live with my aunt, and she can be a bit ... well ... difficult. I don't really like to leave her even when I'm on duty with the WVS, so I'm not sure it would be fair to go out again."

His face lit up.

"Just a quick cuppa?" His eyes begged her again.

"Well, yes, all right. So long as we're not long. There's a café not far from where I live, perhaps we could go there later?"

"We'll go anywhere you like," he said, his eyes now sparkling.

As he walked her home, he told her about his welding apprenticeship in the London Docks and how he wanted to join up, but welders were needed at home to mend the ships and for other vital work. While he chattered about his role as an air raid warden, his job and his family, she was silent – painfully aware of her inexperience with boys. She'd barely seen a male during her time at the convent, let alone held a conversation with one, and since she'd met Kitty and the other girls, who spoke about dances and trips to the cinema with boys, she'd realised how naïve she was.

The closer they got to Aylward Street, the more she regretted accepting his offer of a cup of tea because to him, it obviously meant a lot more than a hot drink. It seemed she'd unwittingly given him the impression they might be more than just friends and she was feeling overwhelmed. It wasn't that she didn't like him – she did. Or at least she liked the warm glow that washed over her every time he looked at her as if he couldn't believe she was with him. But she was out of her depth and if she hadn't felt so tired after the long, harrowing night, she might have been able to think clearly and to extricate herself without hurting his feelings. It was too late now. He took her to Gran's door, shook hands and told her for the third time that he would call for her and he wouldn't be late.

When she'd gone to her bedroom, she peered at her hazy reflection in the old, mottled mirror which hung on the wall. There hadn't been many opportunities to see herself while she'd been at St. Theresa's; Sister Mary Benedicta declaring that vanity was a grave sin. What could Jimmy see when he looked at her so intently? His expression had been one of such admiration, she'd been amazed.

She pulled the ribbon off her ponytail and shook her silky, black hair free to fall over her shoulders. Beneath her straight fringe, enormous eyes stared back at her quizzically. Her skin was a shade or two darker than the other girls she knew, but other than that, she didn't think she looked any different from them – other than for her eyes. At the convent, Sister Mary Benedicta had told her off several times for looking in an insolent manner, but Jimmy had said her eyes were exotic and he'd never seen anything as beautiful.

That evening, Samira told Gran she'd be visiting one of her WVS friends for a short while. At ten to seven, she guiltily slipped out of the house, afraid Jimmy would knock at the door and Gran would see him and realised she'd lied. However, he was already there at the corner when she quietly closed the front door.

"I couldn't wait to see you." He smiled at her, and she wondered if he'd mistaken her early arrival for eagerness to see him.

If only she'd simply told him she couldn't go out to the café with him and then she wouldn't be in such a predicament. How was she supposed to behave? What should she say? What should she *not* say? She simply didn't know, and her stomach was so knotted with nerves, she was sure she wouldn't be able to drink a mouthful of tea. He tucked her arm beneath his as they crossed the road and she fervently hoped he couldn't feel her trembling.

But to her surprise, the time passed quickly – and even more amazingly, she discovered she was enjoying Jimmy's company. He was quick-witted, funny and kind – so easy to be with, and she lost track of time, only remembering at the last minute she'd told Gran she'd be home within the hour. She'd assumed that would be far too long. His face fell when she said she'd have to go home but he gallantly leapt to his feet, paid for their teas, and helped her into her coat.

"When can I see you again?" he asked as they turned into Aylward Street. "How about Thursday afternoon? Are you free?"

She agreed. After all, she'd had a lovely time, but she was acutely aware that in making it so obvious he liked her, he'd placed her under pressure. She wouldn't deliberately hurt him, but it made the possibility of turning down his invitations much harder.

Gran had been upset when Samira had told her she'd be going out for a few hours on Thursday afternoon.

"More training?" she muttered crossly. "Well, make sure you're back by five."

Samira had promised she'd be home on time. She'd then felt guilty at lying, and cross with herself for agreeing to meet Jimmy. Life would be so simple if she'd simply turned him down, but she knew how dejected he would have been had she done so. And anyway, it was flattering he was so obviously smitten with her.

She'd asked him not to knock at the door for her, but in case he forgot, she made sure she was waiting for him outside the house. Mrs Thomsett was standing in her doorway, arms crossed looking up and down the street.

"Afternoon, lovey, you 'aven't seen my Alfie, 'ave you?"

"No, sorry, Mrs Thomsett, I've only just come out."

"Oh well, if you see 'im, tell 'im I'll have his guts for garters if he don't get his backside home immediately."

"I will," said Samira, hoping Jimmy wouldn't arrive before Mrs Thomsett went back in her house.

"Waiting for yer young man, are you?" Mrs Thomsett was in no hurry to leave her doorstep. "That Jimmy McGuire is a lovely lad," she said softly, her eyes warily on Gran's windows.

"How do you know?" Samira was aghast.

"There ain't much I don't know around these parts, lovey."

"You won't tell Mrs Stewart, will you?"

Mrs Thomsett tapped the side of her nose. "Mum's the word. But be careful – she won't like it. I've seen it happen afore with Davey and Amelia. Here's an idea, lovey – ask 'im to meet you around the corner, rather than risk upsetting her." She nodded her roller-clad head at Gran's house.

"And be careful. With this war on, people are living for today and not giving tomorrow much thought. Take my Sally. She's in the family way and her young man's gone off to fight."

"Oh, Mrs Thomsett!" Samira didn't know what to say.

"I know, I know. Sally's always been wilful. But you – you've got a good 'ead on yer shoulders. So, be careful ... and if I was you, I'd start walking down the street right now. Yer young man's just turned the corner."

Despite the unpromising start to the afternoon, Samira thoroughly enjoyed herself. She forgot her guilt at lying to Gran and the shock at knowing her secret had been discovered by Mrs Thomsett – and therefore, probably most of the other women in the street.

They regularly gathered on each other's doorsteps gossiping and it was only that Gran rarely set foot out of the house that meant she hadn't yet heard. Perhaps it was time to tell her, although Mrs Thomsett had suggested otherwise, warning her simply to conceal the truth. Without understanding what her relationship with Jimmy was, it was hard to work out the boundaries. Perhaps it might be best not to tell Gran yet.

Yet? That thought anticipated there was more to come in this friendship with Jimmy, but she felt as if she was riding a runaway horse – it was exhilarating and at the same time frightening.

"And next Wednesday evening, if you're free, I'll take you," he said. "You'll love it."

They were sitting on a bench that encircled a huge tree in the small park in Arbour Square. In front of them, children played on the little patch of lawn that hadn't been given over to growing vegetables.

"Sorry?" she said, ashamed she'd been lost in her own thoughts.

"The dance at the Old Mahogany Bar in Graces Alley. Next Wednesday—"

*"Dance?"* She choked with shock. "Oh no, I couldn't!"

The excitement drained from his face.

"What I mean is," she added gently, "I don't know how to dance, so there's really no point."

"Oh, you don't need to worry about that. We can go early, and I'll show you a few steps. I promise I won't leave your side all night, so you won't be on your own. I'll make sure you enjoy it ..."

How could she get out of it without hurting his feelings?

"Please ..." he said, and she knew the hope in his eyes would be kindled or extinguished depending on her answer.

"Well ..." What could she say?

That was enough for Jimmy.

"I'll pick you up at six and then we'll go in early, and I'll show you a few steps."

She rushed home to arrive before five o'clock so Gran wouldn't have cause to complain and while she spread margarine on slices of bread for tea, the air raid siren began to wail. She sighed.

An evening – and possibly night, under the stairs with Gran wasn't a pleasant prospect.

"We could always go to the Thomsett's Anderson Shelter," Samira suggested although she already knew the answer.

"What! Share a night with that family and all their brats! I don't think so!"

"It was really kind of Mrs Thomsett to ask us."

Gran sniffed. "That's as maybe. But I'd still rather stay here."

When the all-clear sounded, Samira helped her grandmother out of the confined space under the stairs.

"I'm going to bed," Gran announced. "And I don't care how many German aeroplanes come over, I'm not going back in that cupboard tonight."

While Samira cleared away in the kitchen, Mrs Thomsett let herself into the house.

"All okay, lovey?" she asked.

"Yes, thank you. Mrs Stewart's gone to bed with orders not to be disturbed."

"Well, if you ever get fed up cramming yerselves under the stairs, don't forget yer welcome in our shelter."

"Thank you, Mrs Thomsett."

"Yes, I know, lovey, Mrs Stewart wouldn't come into our shelter with my brood if the Jerries were here in the house. I know what she thinks of us, but if you ever want to come. Yer very welcome."

"Thank you."

"Well, out with it!" said Mrs Thomsett, keeping her voice low. "You look as happy as a wet Wednesday. Did your young man upset you?"

"No ... not exactly. But I said I'd go dancing with him next week."

"And that's a problem because ...?"

"I don't really know."

"Right, lovey, let's 'ave a cuppa, and we'll see if we can sort out what's worrying you."

"Well, I'm not exactly worried," said Samira pouring tea into Mrs Thomsett's cup. "I just feel at a bit of a loss. The other girls in the WVS talk about walking out with boys and they seem to have such fun."

"And you don't have fun with Jimmy?"

"Yes, he's good company. He makes me laugh and he seems to care about me."

"Sounds like he's Mr Perfect. So, what's the problem? Ooh, I say, 'e's not pressuring you, is he?" She frowned. "Only if 'e tried that, I'd have his guts fer garters. An' you can tell him I said that. I'd be straight round to see 'is mother and tell her what's what."

"No, no, nothing like that. I suppose it's just I thought it would be different. My parents adored each other – you could tell they were made to be together and sometimes I see Jimmy look at me in a way that tells me he likes me more than I like him. And then I feel bad and wonder why I don't feel the same way."

"Ah! I see." Mrs Thomsett nodded and tapped her lower lip with her forefinger. "Well, everyone's different, of course. But sometimes, love don't always happen neatly. Take my Wilf and me. I met 'im when I were sixteen and I know it's hard to believe it looking at 'im now, but in those days, he were so handsome. I was head over heels in love with 'im – along with most of the other girls in my street. But it took 'im several years before he came around to my way of thinkin'. Sometimes things just move at different speeds. There's nothin' wrong in that. So, why don't you go to yer dance and just enjoy it?"

Samira paused and put the cup down. This was so embarrassing. "The other thing is, I've never been to a dance before. Jimmy says he'll take me early and teach me a few steps but I ... I just feel I'm going to make a fool of myself."

Mrs Thomsett drank the last of her tea, stood up and nodded. "You'll be fine, lovey. Come around tomorrow and I'll get my son,

John, to show you how to waltz. Yer'll pick it up in no time and if you haven't got anything to wear, we'll alter something of Sally's. She's about your size – or she was before she got in the family way. She'll 'ave no need of smart frocks for some time yet."

"I hadn't even thought about what I should wear!" Samira was horrified. "You see. I have no idea."

"You're just young, that's all, an' I don't s'pose the nuns taught you much dancing. Don't worry about it. We all 'ave to start somewhere."

"Thank you so much, Mrs Thomsett. I don't know what I'd do without you."

"Think nothing of it, ducks. We all stick together in this neighbourhood and help each other out when someone's in need. That's what life's all about."

Jimmy switched his torch on briefly every few yards to light their path along Cable Street as they walked to the Old Mahogany Bar. There was no moon to guide them through the blackout, and a heavy mist had descended, making the visibility even worse. Since blackout had been introduced, the incidence of road accidents had increased and he took Samira's hand and held it tightly as they crossed each road, lacing his fingers with hers. He assured her that despite the walk taking longer than he'd anticipated, there'd still be time for her to practise a few dance steps.

As they entered the Old Mahogany Bar, several friends greeted him, and it wasn't until Samira had taken off her hat and coat that Jimmy looked at her for the first time since he'd met her in the dark of Aylward Street.

He gasped and his jaw dropped open.

"Jimmy? What's wrong?" Her cheeks blazed as he stood rooted to the spot, staring at her.

If her legs hadn't gone so weak, she'd have turned and run to save him – and herself – the embarrassment of whatever she'd done that was wrong. Instead, she stood rooted to the spot.

One of his friends nudged him. "Don't tell me this wondrous creature's come with you, you great lummox!"

Jimmy suddenly regained his composure and taking her arm, he said proudly "Yes, she came with me."

"I've never seen anyone as beautiful as you, Samira," he whispered to her as he took her arm and led her to the empty dance floor.

Relief flooded through her as she realised that far from embarrassing him, she seemed to have got everything right, and the uncertainty she'd experienced earlier that evening slowly drained away.

When Samira had announced she was on duty that evening, Gran had believed the lie and for the first time, she'd not complained about being left alone, making Samira feel even more guilty about deceiving her. She'd slipped out of the house in her uniform but instead of setting off down the road, she'd gone next door to number 12. The blue dress Mrs Thomsett had altered for her, fit beautifully, and Sally had pinned her shiny, dark hair up in an elaborate style. They'd told her how wonderful she looked. She hadn't been able to see much in the small mirror Sally held up for her, and she'd left their house assuming they were exaggerating.

Now, Jimmy beamed at her, and she could see how proud he was his friends were envious of his date.

There had been no need for a lesson with Jimmy before the dance began because Mrs Thomsett's son, John, had taught her how to waltz and after a circuit of the hall, her feet began to move automatically to the music without her having to count the beat.

Once the band had tuned their instruments, they struck up their first piece of dance music and other pairs of dancers joined Jimmy and

Samira, gliding and whirling around the hall. When others cut in to take Jimmy's place during the gentleman's excuse-me, he'd glowered from the edge of the dance floor until the opportunity arose to reclaim her. However, he made certain he held her in his arms for the last waltz, taking her hand and leading her away so there'd be no doubt he was the one who would take her home.

The mist had thickened and their progress back to Aylward Street was slow but Samira's earlier nervousness about the dance had been replaced with exhilaration and despite the darkness, she almost felt she could dance home.

When the other WVS girls had talked animatedly of the dances they'd been to, her imagination had failed her. But now she'd experienced the excitement of the rhythm pulsing through her body when she and Jimmy wove between the other couples in the subdued lighting, she understood their enthusiasm.

The blanket of fog felt like a coat of invisibility and Samira allowed Jimmy to take her to Gran's door, knowing they couldn't be seen by the neighbours.

"Would you like to go next Wednesday?" Jimmy asked.

"Yes please," she'd said and taking his hand, she'd raised it above her head and twirled on the spot.

"You're so beautiful, Samira, I could stare into your eyes forever," he whispered, taking her other hand and pulling her close. "I can't believe you're my girl."

For the first time, Samira didn't feel alarmed at his obvious infatuation, although she wasn't sure if it was because she was still caught up in the magic of the evening, or if indeed, she was beginning to feel more than just friendship for him. There was no spark as yet, but it might come.

He put his hands on her shoulders and pulled her closer.

"I'd love to kiss you, Samira," he whispered.

It was enough to break the spell.

Samira drew back in alarm. "No!"

When she thought about it later, she wondered if he'd simply taken her in his arms and kissed her, whether she might have been swept along with the enchantment of the night. But declaring his wish in advance had given her time to be rational – and a shiver of fear had trickled down her spine.

He let go of her and stepped back, horror-stricken. "I ... I didn't mean to upset you or ..." he said anxiously. "I'd never do anything to hurt you ... you know that don't you?"

"I've got to go," she said, slipping into the house and closing the door. She stood with her forehead against the door feeling thoroughly foolish and wondering if Jimmy was still outside.

How could she have been so stupid?

He'd been the perfect gentleman and she'd rudely and childishly rejected him.

If only she'd told him she'd never been kissed before and explained she didn't know what to do, he might have understood. But instead, she'd pushed him away, spoken without thinking and then left him on the doorstep.

Stupid, stupid!

When she got to her bedroom, she looked through the window, but the fog was impenetrable. After such heartless treatment, it was unlikely he'd still be there.

Sitting on the bed, she closed her eyes, touched her lips gently with her fingertip and tried to imagine what it might have been like if he'd simply kissed her. The thought made her feel warm and tingly and she determined the next time she saw Jimmy – assuming he ever talked to her again – she'd find some way of making it up to him and allow him to kiss her properly.

# Chapter Six

S amira looked out for Jimmy each evening when she was on duty with the WVS but despite seeing him in the distance, she hadn't been able to talk to him nor to give him the note she'd written explaining it had been fear which had stopped her kissing him, not disgust, as he might have assumed. She realised with shame how little she knew about him – not even where he lived. He'd been so interested in her, asking questions about her life and she'd never thought to find out about his. When he'd talked about himself, she hadn't listened because she was wondering what to say or do next.

Two weeks after the dance, Samira was on duty. The night was clear, and the moon shone brightly, illuminating the river and the London streets below. The German pilots were taking full advantage of the excellent visibility. They relentlessly attacked the docks with incendiary devices and bombs, starting many fires that took hold in the warehouses and workshops. The rescue services worked furiously to contain the damage and to extinguish the flames, but it seemed like the Luftwaffe weren't going to go home until they'd utterly destroyed their targets.

Samira kept an eye out for Jimmy and although she thought she caught sight of him with another air raid warden, she wasn't certain.

Before she could find out, they were both gone. As the hours passed, fires raged, filling the air with the acrid smell of burning, and with thick, black smoke that stung their eyes. There was no time to think about anything other than helping wherever she could.

The girls were exhausted but determined to remain until they were no longer needed.

"You're doing a great job," Kitty told them, trying to keep their spirits up. "Keep at it! The lads are getting everything under control now, we'll be able to pack up and go home very soon."

But she'd been wrong.

By the time anyone realised the fire had spread to an oil store, it was too late. A tremendous roar rocked the air. Shockwaves so powerful they felt solid, assaulted anything and anyone in their path.

People stopped in their tracks; frozen with shock. As one, they looked up, then staggered backwards away from the scorching heat of the inferno.

Furious, choking, oily flames licked the sky, and as firefighters took in the magnitude of the disaster, shouts filled the air, vying with the crackle of the fire.

Orders. Instructions. Cries for help. Screams of sheer terror.

The roof of a warehouse collapsed in slow motion with a colossal boom, releasing clouds of dust and steam. Again, everyone stopped in horror, then exhausted men suddenly found the strength and determination to renew their efforts. Everyone knew such an enormous disaster would inevitably involve many casualties, and if the fire wasn't contained, it would spread rapidly.

There was only one piece of good news that night. The German pilots could see the docks ablaze, and presumably, believing they'd caused enough havoc for one mission; they'd turned and headed back to the coast and home.

It was hours before the flames were brought under control and a breeze helped to carry the smell of charred wood away down the river. At first, Samira took no notice when she saw Kitty talking to a group of the girls until she realised, they were staring at her, and Mavis was shaking her head sadly. Kitty walked towards her, and the other girls stood silently, watching.

"I'm not sure how to say this, Samira, so I'm just going to come out with it, love. Some of the ARP wardens were trying to put the fire out when it blew. Mavis just saw Tom Riley on a stretcher. I'm afraid he's burned badly. But ... there are three others unaccounted for... and no one knows if your Jimmy was one of them. I'm really sorry." She put her arm around Samira's shoulders. "He still might turn up, of course," she added without much conviction. "Go home, love. Mavis said she'll walk with you ..." She petered out not knowing what else to say.

Samira looked at Kitty, her face expressionless.

"Samira, you understand what I've just told you, don't you?"

"Yes."

As Mavis put her arm around Samira's shoulders and led her away, she turned to Kitty and mouthed *She's in shock. I'll look after her.*

The other girls stood together watching Mavis lead Samira home.

Gran was waiting at the front door when Mavis delivered Samira home.

"Are you all right, Samantha?" she asked eyeing Mavis suspiciously. "Mrs Thomsett told me there's been a terrible accident at the docks. I heard the explosions. I was so worried."

Samira was silent.

"She's fine," said Mavis, "but her friend is believed to have been ..." she mouthed *killed.* "No one's sure what happened but lots of people are missing and—"

Gran stepped forward and drew Samira into the house. "Thank you," she said to Mavis. "Thank you for bringing her home. I'll look after her now."

"Of course," said Mavis, "when she's feeling a bit better, please tell her I'm sorry."

After she'd put Samira to bed, Gran made a cup of sweet tea and took it upstairs.

"Drink it, dear. It'll help with the shock. Then get some sleep. You look exhausted. Things'll be better when you've rested. You'll see."

Samira lay in bed staring at the ceiling.

Missing? What did that mean? Burnt? Crushed beneath a pile of masonry? He'd been so full of life with his jokes and playfulness – sometimes more like a boy than a man. But then he was only eighteen. Her eyes filled with tears, and one spilt out of the corner of her eye. She didn't even know when his birthday was. He'd known about hers and since she'd turned eighteen just before he'd met her, he'd promised the following year, he'd take her somewhere special on her birthday. The night of the 'kiss that never was' replayed in her mind and each time, she sighed and fresh tears spilt on to her pillow. Now she'd never know what his kiss would have felt like.

He'd never asked much of her, how difficult would it have been to allow him just one kiss?

She knew from the shadows on the wall it was late afternoon. Her eyelids were swollen from the smoke, tiredness and tears, but they didn't hurt. She could feel nothing.

Voices drifted up from the hall and she realised it had been the door knocker that had woken her. There was a tap at her door and Mavis anxiously poked her head around it.

"I'm sorry to bother you, Samira, but I've got some news." She hesitated in the doorway. "Can I come in?"

Samira nodded.

"I'm not sure if your aunt knows you were stepping out with Jimmy, so I just told her I had news about a friend who's missing, and she assumed it was one of the WVS girls. But Jimmy's family live around the corner to me and I went to visit his mum earlier. Apparently, he was nowhere near the fire. He's not even in London."

Samira sat up. "Are you sure?"

"Yes, I'm certain."

"Where is he then?"

"He handed in his notice and joined up. There was nothing anyone could do to stop him. He's left for training camp, but Mrs McGuire didn't know where. She was furious he was giving up his apprenticeship, so he went without telling her where he was going. But he left this letter for you. I'm afraid his mother was so upset he'd gone, she opened it to see if he'd told you where he was going."

"And did it say?"

Mavis shook her head. "No. It was very wrong of her to open it, but now she has, she blames you for Jimmy going away. I'm really sorry, Sam but you feel better knowing he's still alive ... don't you?"

Samira nodded and took the letter.

"Well, I'll leave you to read it," said Mavis turning to go. "I'm glad he's all right, although I suppose it depends on where he gets stationed as to how long he remains safe. Anyway, Kitty says to take your time before you come back."

When Mavis had gone, Samira slowly took the single sheet of paper out of the torn envelope.

*My dearest Samira,*

*I'm sorry to go away without saying goodbye but I think it's for the best. I suppose you know I've loved you from the first time I ever saw you. But I also know you're much too good for me. Thank you for being kind but I could see in your eyes you didn't feel the same way. It was foolish of me to hope. Anyway, I'm sorry for upsetting you after the dance but you were so lovely it took my breath away, I could have stared into your eyes forever, and I suppose I got carried away. I hope you can forgive me. I can't bear to be near you and know you'll never be mine, so I'm leaving and by the time you read this, I will be at training camp, possibly even out of the country. I'm looking forward to being a soldier and travelling. I reckon it will make a man of me. Perhaps one day we'll meet again and I'll be the sort of man you might fall for.*

*With all my love,*

*Jimmy*

Tears slipped through Samira's swollen eyelids as she slowly folded the letter and tucked it back in the envelope. At least he was still alive. She wondered how his mother must feel knowing that he'd thrown away the chance of his apprenticeship and gone away because of her.

Would it have been so hard to love him as he'd loved her?

She closed her eyes and tried to bring Jimmy's face to mind but the harder she searched for him, the fainter his image became.

Did that spark she imagined she needed before she could give her heart, really exist? Or had she just ruined her chances of having a kind, loving and sweet man?

# Chapter Seven

The aerial bombardment of London intensified during the weeks after the night of the great fire in the docks. Samira didn't like to think of Gran on her own under the stairs during the nights when she was on duty and suggested she either go to the Underground station overnight or to the Thomsett's Anderson Shelter.

"Do you know how early the queues start before anyone's allowed down the Tube station at four o'clock? Some people are there all day. I'm not standing around for hours just so I can cram myself between some unsavoury people on a train platform. And don't ask me to go next door with that rabble. I'd rather die in my bed."

But surprisingly, Gran had taken notice of Samira's fears and although she hadn't done as she'd suggested, she had paid Mr Thomsett and two of his sons to build an Anderson Shelter in her backyard. Samira wasn't entirely happy with her grandmother being on her own anywhere, but despite being damp and cold, at least it was possible to stretch out and sleep if the noise of the bombs allowed – something that was not so easily done under the stairs.

To take her mind off Jimmy, Samira had thrown herself into her voluntary work with the WVS. She'd taken over driving the van because Kitty had lacerated both hands when rescuing a child who'd been buried in rubble. As well as serving food and drinks to the rescue servicemen and women, Samira helped evacuate hundreds of young London children, sending them to parts of the country which were less likely to be attacked by the Luftwaffe. Most of the time she was too busy, or too tired, to think about Jimmy but occasionally, she'd see an ARP warden of similar build and height to him in the distance and it would bring back the evening of the fire when she thought he'd died.

She'd heard he'd been stationed somewhere near the French-Belgian border, but Mavis didn't know more than that – and if she did, she wasn't telling.

Samira had concluded something was lacking in her character which meant she couldn't fall in love. Or perhaps she was just too emotionally immature. If she'd had a mother, she'd have discussed it with her, but there was no one she trusted enough to ask. She came close to asking Mrs Thomsett once or twice, but embarrassment made her draw back. In the meantime, she turned down any offers of dates or outings, and concentrated on her WVS duties, and on caring for Gran.

One morning as she returned to Aylward Street after a particularly busy night, she'd been surprised Gran hadn't been in the kitchen waiting for her. The all-clear had been given hours before and usually, Gran didn't hesitate to leave the damp Anderson Shelter and make for the kitchen to put the kettle on. Samira climbed the stairs and hesitated outside her grandmother's door. Perhaps she hadn't bothered to leave her bed when the air raid siren had sounded, and she was still fast asleep. Samira tapped gently and opened the door, but Gran's bed had not been slept in. On shaky legs, Samira ran down the stairs, and out into the backyard. She held her breath as she threw open the door of the Anderson Shelter. Inside, lying on the bunk, Gran lay gasping for breath, clutching her heart. Large, fearful eyes set in an ashen face blinked in the light.

Samira helped her from the shelter and shouted for assistance as she half-carried Gran back to the house. Mrs Thomsett came rushing in, followed by several young children who stood by the kitchen door with wide eyes and open mouths.

"Bertie, run down to the Post Office and tell Mrs Higgins we need Dr Jenkins fer Mrs Stewart! Now! The rest of you, stop yer gawping. Go and get yer Pa."

The children turned and scampered down the hall. Samira wiped the sweat from her grandmother's face with a damp cloth, holding her hand and speaking gently to calm her. She was still grey, but her eyes no longer registered such fear although they bulged with the effort of drawing sufficient air into her lungs. Samira's words seemed to calm her, and gradually, Gran's breathing became less laboured.

When Mr Thomsett arrived, he carried Gran gently up the stairs to her bed and Samira and Mrs Thomsett settled her. They'd just finished making her comfortable when Dr Jenkins arrived, and he asked them to wait outside.

"Don't fret so, lovey." Mrs Thomsett placed a hand on Samira's shoulder. "Dr Jenkins'll soon have 'er as right as rain. Even her colour's better now than when I first saw her. She were positively grey. But she'll be all right. Now, I'll put the kettle on. I expect she'll be demanding a cuppa any minute now. You see if she don't."

When Dr Jenkins allowed Samira back upstairs with a cup of tea, Gran was sitting up in bed and a little colour had returned, although she was still pale. Her breathing was normal, and she smiled weakly when she saw Samira.

Dr Jenkins handed Samira a prescription. "This is for Mrs Stewart. I'm insisting she has bed rest while she can. If the sirens go, you'll have to help her down to the shelter and stay with her. Or even better, make her up a bed downstairs. I'll call back tomorrow and see how she is. But it's important she remains calm – well, as much as anyone can during this dreadful war. Her heart isn't strong, as you know, but she seems to have a strong constitution. No reason why she shouldn't carry on for ages – so long as she takes my advice. Well, I'll bid you good day. It seems half of Stepney has need of me this morning." He snapped the clasp of his briefcase shut and hurried out of the bedroom.

"That was quite a scare you gave me," said Samira with a smile.

"Thank you for your quick thinking, Samantha. You saved my life." Gran craned her neck to see around Samira. "Is Mrs Thomsett still here?"

"No, everyone's gone."

"Are you sure?"

"Yes, I saw them go before I came up to see you. Do you want to speak to her?"

"No! I just wanted to make sure she'd gone. I need to tell you something and I don't want that busybody to know." Gran paused and allowed her breathing to calm down.

"Samantha, I want you to open my wardrobe door and look inside on the left. You'll find a hatbox under a few other things. There's a biscuit tin in there. I want you to bring it to me."

Samira lifted the hatbox out of the wardrobe and placing it on the bed, she pulled off the lid. After taking out four identical, black, velvet evening bags decorated with jet beads she saw the two faded bluebirds on the lid of an octagonal biscuit tin. When she lifted it out of the hatbox, it was surprisingly heavy and at Gran's instruction, she prised the lid off to reveal rolls of banknotes and an assortment of trinkets.

"Nobody knows about this box, Samantha. Just you and me. It's my insurance but I may not need it much longer—"

"What do you mean? The doctor said if you rest, you'll be fine," said Samira aghast.

"He's an old fool. He might be right, and he might be wrong, but I need to know you'll take this if he's wrong and anything happens to me. I don't want anyone else to have it. You're a good girl and you deserve good things to happen to you but what we deserve and what we get are not always the same. You're young and you don't have the experience I have, but take my word for it, in the end, you have to look out for yourself. People will come into your life and people will leave, but trust me, they'll let you down and, in the end, you'll be alone. The only thing you can do is make sure you've got enough to keep yourself. There's money in here for my funeral but you must keep the rest. Sell the other pieces if you need to ..." She picked up a silver-framed photograph of a baby and a pearl brooch. "I don't suppose they'll bring much but it all helps. Here's my wedding ring," she said, holding it up between finger and thumb. "It's gold, so it'll raise something. But don't tell anyone about this. You can't trust anyone, d'you hear?"

She sank back the pillows, her face pale and drawn.

"Please don't talk like that. You'll soon be back to normal." Samira repacked the tin, placed it back in the hatbox which she put in the wardrobe.

"Promise you'll do as I ask." Gran's voice was faint but determined.

"Yes, of course. Now please rest. I'm going to go to the chemist to get your medicine. Would you like me to call Mrs Thomsett and ask her to sit with you while I'm gone?"

Gran wearily shook her head. "No, I'll just have a sleep while you're out. Perhaps we could have some tea when you get back?"

Samira ran to the chemist shop, waited patiently until the medicine was ready and then hurried back to Aylward Street. She knocked on Gran's door but there was no reply, so she quietly let herself in. Gran was lying as Samira had left her but her eyes although open, were unseeing, and her chest which had previously been rising and falling with the exertion of breathing, was still. The fingers of each hand were splayed as if she'd been reaching towards the box in the wardrobe. Or perhaps she'd wanted to remind Samira of her last wishes.

# Chapter Eight

♥

The undertaker straightened his top hat, checked the coffin was steady on the pallbearers' shoulders and turned to lead the procession into the church.

"Are you all right?" Pop asked, taking Samira's arm.

She nodded. "I've never been to a funeral before ..."

"It'll be fine, you'll see," he said holding open the enormous wooden, church door for her.

If Samira hadn't spotted Mrs Thomsett sitting at the back, she'd have thought they were taking her grandmother's coffin into the wrong church. As far as Samira knew, Gran hadn't had any friends, so she was amazed to see so many people at the funeral service. She recognised Joanna sitting next to a handsome man – presumably her husband, Ben. Next to her, was a vivacious-looking woman who turned and smiled at Pop.

He gasped and waved at her. "It's Amelia!" he whispered to Samira. "Oh, my dear! She came."

Pop's daughter, Amelia, was sitting with a man and young girl – presumably her husband and daughter – the young girl was a miniature version of her mother. Several neighbours from Aylward Street flanked Mrs Thomsett, and tears began to fill Samira's eyes as she realised people had bothered to show respect to a woman who'd been less than friendly to them.

On the other side of the aisle, an attractive woman sat alone, hands in her lap, watching Pop intently. Samira knew from a photograph Pop had shown her that she was his mistress, Edie.

In front of her, there was an older man and Pop stopped to shake hands with him. "Thanks for coming Pete," he whispered. Next to him, was a young couple. The woman was smartly dressed in a dark, grey suit and matching hat, and from his uniform, Samira could see the man belonged to the Royal Air Force. She didn't know anyone called Pete and assumed he and the young couple were friends of Pop. As she moved further forward, she looked back at the group and realised the couple were probably her age and bore an uncanny resemblance to each other with their blonde hair and good looks.

Samira and Pop slid into the front pew on their own, while the coffin was being settled on a plinth and she half-turned to get a better look at the young couple. She'd never seen such a handsome man and it wasn't until she saw the girl smiling at her, she realised she'd been staring.

With glowing cheeks, she turned away and busied herself looking through the hymn book. The girl had an air of sophistication, perfectly groomed and effortlessly fashionable. Samira wished she was wearing something more glamorous than one of Gran's dresses which Mrs Thomsett had altered for her.

*This is your grandmother's funeral, not a fashion show.*

She sat rigidly, staring at the altar, determined not to glance behind her again.

With a large, black bible tucked under his arm, Reverend Pettifer walked up the steps into the pulpit. He appeared to know very little about Gran – not surprisingly because as far as Samira knew, she'd never been a churchgoer – but the service was as personal as if he'd been reading out a shopping list.

Perhaps all funerals are like this?

Samira had the impression from those of the WVS girls who'd lost family members, there was a great outpouring of grief at funerals. Glancing around, she didn't see anyone dabbing eyes or looking anything other than dutiful – or bored. Samira supposed that wasn't surprising really – it was enough that people had bothered to come to the funeral of the woman who'd ultimately driven many of them away.

The eulogy was brief, unsentimental and devoid of detail, but Samira decided Gran would probably have approved and been grateful that her life – and her death were private matters.

"Amen," said Reverend Pettifer bowing his head briefly as he concluded the service. He closed his bible and ran his gaze over the congregation until it reached Edie and then moved to Pop. His expression hardened. He glared for several seconds, then gathering his robes, he climbed down the steps of the pulpit with his bible under his arm. Signalling to the pallbearers to raise the coffin, he led them into the graveyard for the burial. When Samira thought about it later, she could remember very little about what happened at the graveside other than everyone huddling around the hole in the ground, shivering in the unseasonal, bitter wind that had threatened to freeze the tears on her cheeks.

Finally, the funeral service was concluded, and the mourners walked back to the path out of the churchyard, leaving the gravediggers to fill the deep hole with earth. Reverend Pettifer stopped briefly to speak to Edie and then clutching his enormous bible to his chest, he strode back to the church without a backward glance.

Edie's cheeks had turned crimson and instantly, her face changed from attractive, to petulant. Pop had been introducing Samira to

Amelia and her husband and hadn't noticed the change in Edie until she marched up to him. She took his arm, insisting she have a word with him.

Although Samira hadn't intended to eavesdrop, she was standing close enough to hear snatches of heated conversation, which included the words *vicar* and *living in sin* and *married* and *widower*.

"Now's not the time, Edie, we'll talk about it later," Pop said leading her away, but Samira knew he was angry and judging by Amelia's expression, so was she.

"What a cheek that woman's got! How my father could put up with her rudeness, I just don't know. He's never had much sense with women," she said. "First Mum, who wasn't the easiest person to get on with, and then that creature. I know I didn't get on with my mother, but she was worth ten of that spoilt woman. How dare she try to persuade my father to marry her just because the vicar told her off for living in sin. At my mother's funeral too."

"Very bad form," said Will, her husband, nodding in agreement.

"What's very bad form?" asked Joanna, who'd caught up with Samira, to introduce her husband, Ben.

"Never mind," said Amelia hugging Joanna. "Let's not worry about Edie. How are you, darling? You're looking wonderful!"

"I'm fine, thanks, Amelia. And I see you've met your niece at last." she put her arm around Samira's shoulders. "How are you, darling? We've been so worried about you with all the bombing raids on the East End. Thanks for phoning regularly and keeping us updated with your news. I'd have loved to have visited you but ..." She shrugged. "It would only have upset Aunt Ivy. You must be an angel to have charmed her. Now she's gone, I expect you're feeling a bit lost."

"Well, I definitely wouldn't describe myself as an angel. It is strange though. I can't believe she's gone. There is one thing that bothers me

– sometimes she treated me like a carer, paid for by Pop. But much of the time, she treated me like a granddaughter. I wish I knew the truth. I should have asked her ..."

"Aunt Ivy was a very secretive person. Perhaps she didn't even want to admit to herself she knew who you were. But I don't suppose she'd have told you if you'd asked. She obviously enjoyed having you with her – whether she knew who you were or not."

"She was definitely one of a kind," said Amelia. "And I think you deserve a medal, Samira. I couldn't have lived in the same house as her. She was impossible. But let's forget past squabbles, I want to know all about you. Will's going to drive you and me back to Aylward Street, and you can tell us all about what my big brother, Davy, has been up to in India."

Gran's kitchen was full of people and Samira found herself redundant. Despite the food rationing, there was an enormous spread of food on the table in Gran's kitchen and Mrs Thomsett stood guard, making sure the family had plenty to eat before the neighbours helped themselves – especially the children who were hiding beneath the table. Amelia and Joanna poured and served tea and Pop had taken a sulking Edie into the backyard to talk in private. Samira felt like a stranger, in what she'd almost come to consider, her home.

"Ah, at last. I've got you to myself." It was the sophisticated girl who'd been sitting with the man Pop had greeted as Pete and the young man in the RAF uniform.

"I'm Alexandra Jackson but my friends call me Lexie and I know who you are." She shook hands with Samira. "It's lovely to meet you. I've heard all about how you looked after Ivy. Of course, I never met her, but Granddad Peter has told me a few stories!"

"Granddad Peter?"

"Oh, I'm so silly, you probably have no idea who I am."

She was interrupted by a cry of "Ow! Ow!" as Mrs Thomsett dragged two small boys by the backs of their collars away from the table.

"You've 'ad enough! Show some manners and leave some fer yer betters!" She marched the lads to the front door.

"Is there somewhere we could go to talk?" asked Lexie. "It would be lovely to get to know each other better, especially if we're to be housemates."

"Housemates?" Samira began to feel foolish, so far, she'd said nothing except echo Lexie's words.

"Oh no! I'm so sorry, sometimes I have such a big mouth. Joanna hasn't asked you yet, has she? And I think your grandfather probably has more pressing matters on his mind after the vicar lectured his lady friend on the virtues of marriage. Honestly, darling, you should have heard him. He said their domestic arrangements were thoroughly sinful and she now had the chance to redeem herself. But of course, she's got to convince your grandfather first. I heard every word because I sidled up to listen. Although heaven only knows how the vicar knows who Edie is. One of Ivy's neighbours must have spilt the beans ..."

Samira couldn't help liking the girl. Her blonde hair was brushed back off her face in victory rolls and with her porcelain skin and blue eyes, she reminded Samira of a doll. But when she smiled, she had a mischievous air.

"Let's go to my bedroom and talk," Samira said, "that is if we can get out of this crush." They squeezed through the crowd in the kitchen and hall, and Samira led Lexie upstairs.

"I swear there are more people downstairs than there were in the church," said Lexie.

Samira laughed, "Yes, word's obviously got out around there's food on offer."

"Isn't that rather a liberty?"

"No, not really. Pop knows how kind the neighbours have been to me. And they would have been good to Gran too, if she'd let them. Many of them have such large families, they struggled before the war but now, with rationing, they're finding it hard to make ends meet."

Samira opened the bedroom door for Lexie and motioned for her to sit on the bed. The elegant girl looked completely out of place in her bedroom and Samira wondered why she'd never noticed the sagging mattress, the threadbare counterpane, and the wardrobe with the broken door.

Life in St. Theresa's couldn't have been described as luxurious and she was used to shabbiness, but now with Lexie sitting on her bed, she saw the room through different eyes. She looked down at Gran's cast-off, plain navy dress which was reminiscent of a school gymslip and then at Lexie's dark grey suit and white shirt with a bow at the neck. But more than the clothes, Lexie glowed with confidence, Samira thought she would still have looked marvellous dressed in a sack.

"So," said Lexie. "Firstly, I ought to tell you how we're related. Joanna's parents, Rose and Tom, are both dead but Tom was my Granddad Peter's brother. Your granddad is Rose's brother. So, we're only related by marriage, but Granddad Peter spent a lot of time with Rose and Tom before Joanna was born and he knew them very well. When he bought a farm in Devon, he saw less of them but always kept in touch."

Samira suddenly realised she hadn't seen Lexie's grandfather in the house, nor the handsome RAF man.

As if reading her thoughts, Lexie added "I hope you don't mind but Granddad's gone home. He was very nervous about coming up to London with all the bombing, but he wanted to pay his respects at the church. Once he'd done that, he decided he'd go home to Devon tonight rather than stay with Joanna, as planned. Granddad fought in the Great War with Tom and although they came back, they both had shell shock and never really got over what they'd experienced in northern France. You didn't get a chance to meet my twin, Luke; he's taken Granddad to the station. He'll be back later – I'll introduce you both then."

"So, what's this about us being housemates?"

"Well, that's if you want to be, of course. Joanna is going to suggest you stay with her in Essex. It'll get you out of London and all the air raids. I'm going to stay with her too."

"That would be wonderful. I was planning on getting a job or joining up and renting a room somewhere. Pop asked me if I'd like to carry on living here rent-free, but Edie wants him to either sell it or find tenants. I don't want to be the cause of problems for Pop and anyway, I'm not sure I want to live here now Gran's gone."

"Marvellous! I'll tell Joanna! Come tonight. Luke'll be there too. He's going to be stationed at RAF Hornchurch, but he's got two days leave."

Samira's heart beat faster and she could suddenly see Luke's face clearly in her imagination – his short hair, the same colour as Lexie's and the smile which lit up his face. It was all very well having a crush on someone from afar, but she feared she'd make a fool of herself if they were staying in the same house. She had no idea how to behave with men – Jimmy had shown her that – and for some reason, she knew she'd have even less idea how to behave with Luke. It would probably be best to wait until he'd gone to Hornchurch – assuming Joanna asked her to stay, of course. Yes, it would be best to wait for an invitation.

"Will Joanna have enough room for us all?" she asked.

"Oh yes, her house is enormous. Ben's parents were wealthy landowners, so don't worry about that."

When all the neighbours had left, Pop told Edie there were several things he needed to sort out and to pack up, so they'd be staying in the house at least overnight. Edie's mother was looking after their daughters, so they had no need to rush home and he wanted a chance to make sure Samira was happy too.

Making her point with a finger jabbing Pop's chest, Edie said she wouldn't stay in Ivy's house overnight under any circumstances and demanded he take her home. When Pop told her he intended to stay and if she didn't like it, she could return on the train on her own, her mouth set in a rigid line.

Pop had looked appealingly at Amelia and Will who were about to leave in their motor car, and picking up the silent signal, Amelia had offered to take Edie to the station.

"Thank you, Amelia," he'd whispered in her ear when he'd kissed her goodbye. "I owe you."

Edie had stomped to the car and got in the front passenger seat without checking where Amelia wanted to sit.

"She gets travel sick in the back seat," said Pop apologetically.

"Dad, you need to stand up to that woman. Honestly! She's so spoilt."

Pop and Samira waved them off and went back into the kitchen to do the last of the tidying up.

"Let's have a cup of tea, love, and talk about the future," said Pop putting the kettle on the stove. "Are you happy about living with Joanna and Ben? Because just say the word and you can stay here. I'll pay for everything – you don't need to worry about that. And you don't need to worry about what Edie wants either. I know I've got to be a bit stronger with her ... and I will." His shoulders slumped.

Poor Pop. He was such a nice man, but he seemed to be drawn to much stronger women.

"Anyway, I want you to be happy – and safe, of course. So just say what you'd like to do."

"Thanks, Pop. I think I'd like to go to the country. Now Gran's not here, I don't think I want to stay in this house. Joanna said she or Ben would come and fetch me on Thursday at midday, so I've got two days to pack up my things."

"All right, love. And remember, Ivy left everything to you in her will, so you won't be penniless."

"I'm so sorry Pop, whatever she had, really belongs to you. I feel awful."

"Don't be silly, love. I forfeited my right to anything Ivy owned several years ago when I walked out."

Samira was silent for a moment wondering if she ought to tell him about the box in her grandmother's room. But what harm could it do Gran now? "Pop, there's something I need to show you. Gran didn't want me to tell anyone, but I'd feel bad if I kept it to myself."

Samira went upstairs and returned a few minutes later with Gran's hatbox. Taking the octagonal biscuit tin out from amongst the black evening bags, she put it on the table in front of Pop.

"Ah! Ivy's tin. I knew she hid money and things in it. I came across it once when she used to hide it in the scullery. If she wanted you to have it, then take it, love. No, don't open it. I don't want to see what's inside. You keep the tin and do what you like with the contents, they're yours." He patted Samira's hand. "But you might want to show those evening bags to Joanna when you get to her house, they look like they might have been her mother's. They're just the sort of thing she used to make to sell, and I can't think why Ivy should have so many of them. One I can understand, but not four."

"Now," he said and yawned. "It's been a long and difficult day, so I'm going to try to get some sleep. I'll stay down here on the armchair – I can't bear the thought of spending any time in Ivy's bed. Tomorrow, we'll sort the house out and put the word around to try to find some tenants. There are plenty of people who need housing at the moment, so we shouldn't find it hard to rent the house out."

It hadn't taken Samira long to pack her belongings, but she'd spent a lot of time saying goodbye to Kitty and the other WVS girls, and to Mrs Thomsett and the neighbours in the road.

"Look after yerself, Samira," said Mrs Thomsett. "And don't forget to come back and visit before yer go off home to foreign parts, if that's what you plan to do. Yer a lovely girl and Mrs Stewart was lucky to have had you. Yer our little bit of exotic in dull old Stepney."

Samira's cases were in the hall to load into Joanna's car. She wanted to spend a few minutes in her bedroom trying to reconnect with the life she'd known with the grandmother she'd never had the chance to call *Gran* or *Nan* or indeed, anything less formal than *Mrs Stewart*.

Samira stood with her hands on the windowsill, looking down at the children playing in the cobbled street. This would be the last time she'd see this view – tomorrow, she'd wake to … what? Fields? A garden? She had no idea. Was this strange ache she was experiencing, sorrow at leaving London or anxiety at an unknown future? It seemed like neither – it was just an emptiness waiting for something meaningful to fill it. The day after Gran had died, she'd noticed a small, colourful bird perched in a bush in the backyard and had thrown out some stale crumbs of bread for it. When it had seen her, it had flown into the tree and watched until she'd gone back inside, then it had soared down to land on the roof of the Anderson Shelter, looking at the scraps. The brilliant plumage stood out against the brown earth, and she realised it was a budgerigar – probably a pet that had escaped during a bombing raid. For some time, it watched the food from the shelter roof, its head swivelling left and right as if afraid to take a chance on the crumbs. Samira wished she'd thrown the bread closer to the shelter, but it was too late now. She knew if she opened the door, the nervous bird would simply fly away hungry. Having been fed all its life, it was probably struggling in the wild. Then, perhaps hunger or rashness drove it to swoop down to the grass and to peck at the bread. Within seconds, two sparrows joined it, jostling each other for a meal and the budgerigar flew off. Samira stopped herself from shooing the sparrows away – after all, it wasn't their fault the budgie was afraid. Life in a cage hadn't prepared it for survival in the wild.

After that, Samira kept an eye out for the colourful bird, but it had never reappeared and she assumed it hadn't been able to adapt to a world where it didn't belong. How similar she was to that budgie. She wasn't as noticeably different from her neighbours as the budgerigar was from the wild birds. Or perhaps she was. Mrs Thomsett's words came back to her *You're a little bit of exotic in dull old Stepney.* They were meant to be kindly words, she was sure, but despite living in the same street, wearing a WVS uniform and thinking she'd been assimilated into the community, it appeared she was still perceived as being different, as if she didn't belong. But would she fit in any better at Joanna's? Would she ever find a place to call home?

One of the girls in the street dropped her skipping rope and pointed excitedly. The other children turned to see what had caught her attention and began to run towards the car which had turned into Aylward Street. Samira sighed and with one last glance around the empty room, she went downstairs. Pop was waiting in the hall next to her bags, ready to carry them out to the car. His face fell when he saw her tears.

"Have you changed your mind about going? It's not too late to stay. I'll put the new tenants off. Just say the word."

"No, no, Pop, it's all right. I'm fine – really. I just don't like goodbyes, that's all." How could she tell him she was upset because she didn't feel she belonged anywhere? What would be the point of telling him? There was nothing he could do about it.

Pop opened the door and there on the doorstep, just about to knock, was Luke.

Samira's heart sank. What on earth was she going to say to him? But Joanna was very chatty, perhaps she would do most of the talking on the way home. And possibly they'd drop Luke off at Hornchurch so she wouldn't have to endure the whole journey with him to Laindon.

Luke smiled at them. "Joanna sends her apologies, but her son's been up with earache all night and she's waiting for the doctor to call, so I volunteered to come and fetch you."

"That's very kind of you, Luke," said Pop. "Isn't it, Samira?" he added, filling the silence.

"Er, yes, yes, thank you." Samira bent down to pick up her bags to hide her flaming cheeks.

"Allow me." Luke stepped into the hall to pick up her bags.

Pop opened his arms to hug her.

"Luke seems like a nice young man," he whispered to her as she clung to him. "Now, keep in touch. Joanna has a telephone, and I'll try to call as often as I can, so I know you're all right. I haven't heard from your father recently. Have you?"

"No, I've written several times to tell him I'm going to Joanna's, but I haven't had a reply. I've sent several letters to Vikash too."

"I'm sure they're all right, love. Anyway, it looks like Luke's ready to leave. Now, don't worry if you've forgotten anything, it'll give me a wonderful excuse to visit you."

He held out a handkerchief to Samira. "I always seem to be here when you're upset because you're saying goodbye," he said with a sigh.

"But at least you're here," said Samira, she held the handkerchief to her nose, breathing in the smell of pipe tobacco, leather and his spicy cologne. She kissed his cheek. "I would feel worse if I was alone."

He took her hand to kiss it, but she pulled it away and turned her cheek towards him. "When you left me here that first day, you said you wouldn't kiss me on the cheek because we were little more than strangers and that one day when we were really grandfather and granddaughter, you would. Can that day be today?"

There were tears in his eyes when he kissed her gently on the cheek.

# Chapter Nine

C hildren ran alongside the car shouting their farewells as it pulled away from the kerb, and one of Mrs Thomsett's grandsons threw a dandelion through the window which landed in Samira's lap. She looked over her shoulder and watched them stop at the corner waving. The car picked up speed along Jamaica Street and left them behind.

"You seem to have made a good impression on the local children." Luke smiled at her. "The journey'll take a while, why don't you tell me about your life here. You were the only person who showed the slightest emotion at the funeral, so I assume Ivy meant a great deal to you?"

She started diffidently at first. Of course, he wasn't really interested in her. Yet, each time she paused, he asked her something that showed he'd been listening intently. He didn't pry, and if she hesitated, he didn't press her, but he knew exactly what to say to put her at ease. To her surprise, she told him about her life with Gran, her time at the convent school and her early life in India. Before she knew it, they were approaching Romford.

How rude he must think her, talking about herself for so long.

"But tell me about you," she said. "Lexie told me you live in Devon."

"We used to. But I don't suppose either of us will ever go back. It's a beautiful place but our farm's rather remote, and Lex and I felt a bit isolated. It suits our parents though. Granddad moved down there after he came back from the Great War looking for somewhere quiet after the horrors he'd seen in the trenches. Mother was about fourteen when they moved there, and luckily, she loves the solitude, but for some reason, Lexie and I have always looked for something more exciting. I suppose that's why I joined the RAF and trained as a pilot."

"You're so brave. I'd be scared stiff. I'm too much of a coward to fly in an aeroplane."

"Flying's something I've longed to do since I was a young boy. Lex and I used to dream about the places we'd visit in our own private aeroplane. We longed to go to India. It seemed so mysterious and exciting. How lucky you are to have lived there."

"It just seemed normal when I was there." This wasn't how she'd thought the journey would be when she'd realised Luke would be driving her. At first, she'd been frozen with embarrassment, imagining he'd consider spending time with her a chore. But he'd somehow made her sound interesting, as if he envied her.

Luke halted to allow a woman pushing a pram to cross the road. "If you don't mind, I'd like to stop off near the airfield at Hornchurch. I've been staying with a friend, and I left some photographs at his house which I promised Joanna I'd show her. It won't take long, and you might get to see some of the aircraft take off. It's a wonderful sight."

"Yes, I'd love that." Samira relaxed even further. The landscape was like the Kentish countryside around St. Theresa's Convent, and it was familiar and welcoming. She hadn't felt so carefree and content for a long time. In fact, she couldn't ever remember feeling as happy as she was now watching the countryside glide past with Luke at the wheel manoeuvring the car as if it was an extension of his body. If he announced he wanted to keep driving to John O'Groats, she'd have been thrilled.

Glancing at Luke's hand resting on the gear stick, she wondered what it would be like to hold it, to have his long fingers laced with hers. She observed him out of the corner of her eye, keeping her head facing forward in case he noticed her stare. Her breath caught in her throat – even in profile, he was handsome. She'd been too embarrassed to make eye contact with him when he'd introduced himself at Gran's house after the funeral, so she hadn't noticed his crystal blue eyes but now, she watched with fascination as they took in the road ahead and checked the rear-view mirror. As he concentrated on the road and the increasing numbers of pedestrians on the approach to the centre of Hornchurch, she couldn't tear her gaze away from him.

"Can you see the horns up there?" he asked pointing up at the roof of St. Andrew's Church. "It's a bull's skull. That's not something you often see on top of a church."

His words and the movement of his arm jerked her out of her reverie, and she hoped he wouldn't notice the heightened colour of her cheeks.

"Archie's house is a bit further on along the High Road, then off to the left, so it's not far now. Are you hot? I can open the window a bit if you like."

"No, I'm fine, thanks," she said, her blush deepening. She pretended to be preoccupied with the dandelion in her lap and with her head low, she willed the colour in her cheeks to fade.

Luke pulled up outside a large, detached house and turned the engine off.

"Would you like to come in?" he asked. "I won't be a minute, but you might like to stretch your legs."

Samira was about to accept when she saw a woman waving from the doorstep of Archie's house.

"Darling!" she shouted, hurrying down the path towards the gate. "Why didn't you tell me you were coming?"

Luke got out of the car and the woman flew towards him and wrapped her arms around his neck. They were standing so close to the car window; Samira couldn't see their heads but their bodies were pressed together and she could see hands with perfectly-manicured red nails on the small of Luke's back. He laughed and reaching behind, took one of her hands then led her up the path into the house.

Samira let go of the door handle. Luke seemed to have forgotten about her.

Well, what had she expected? That he would fall for such a young, inexperienced girl when he clearly had stylish women ready to throw themselves into his arms? She might have left St. Theresa's Convent, but she still had the air of a schoolgirl, with her simple dress and shoes, and her hair worn long and straight. The woman who'd greeted Luke was probably not much older than Samira, but her dusky pink suit was nipped in at the waist giving her an hourglass figure and the matching hat sat at just the right angle to show off the curls and waves of her blonde hair. Samira had only caught a glimpse of the woman's face, but it was enough for her to notice the woman's lips were bright red, a shade that matched her nail polish, and Samira had no doubt the rest of her face was impeccably made up too.

She looked down at the dandelion that she'd cradled carefully in her hands all the way from Stepney. How childish! She was sure *that* woman wouldn't be seen anywhere near a dandelion unless it was growing in the grass she was walking on. No, she'd have colourful orchids or vases full of red roses. Samira opened the car door a fraction and dropped the yellow flower onto the road. She didn't want any reminders of this car journey which had been so enjoyable and had made her feel special. It had raised her hopes and then dashed them.

*Hopes? Hopes of what?* No one had promised her anything, she'd simply fooled herself. And that thought made her even more angry with herself. Luke was simply a kind, socially experienced man who'd taken the trouble to make the journey more pleasant than it might have been had they travelled in silence. And she was a stupid schoolgirl who'd allowed herself to entertain romantic ideas about a man who couldn't possibly have any interest in her.

When she heard the front door open, she stared resolutely at her lap. She didn't want to see the woman again.

"See you Saturday, darling," the woman called as Luke climbed into the car. He turned and placed a photograph album on the back seat.

Samira couldn't help herself. She glanced at the woman standing by the gate blowing kisses as Luke started the engine and eased the car away from the kerb.

"That was Vera, Archie's sister. Sorry, I'd have introduced you to her, but it was hard to get a word in edgeways. By the time I realised you weren't behind me, it was too late. I'm sure you'll meet her again. I'll introduce you properly then."

The lump in Samira's throat wouldn't allow her to reply.

He looked at her quizzically. "What happened to your dandelion?"

She finally managed to say, "It wilted. I threw it away."

# Chapter Ten

L uke pointed out several Spitfires taking off from the RAF airfield and related some of his experiences since he'd joined the force. She couldn't help feeling it was like being out with an uncle who was reluctantly trying to entertain a niece. She knew that wasn't a fair analogy because he hadn't altered from when they'd left Stepney. Any change that had taken place, had been in her. Furthermore, she had no right to feel let down because it was clear there'd never be anything between a handsome, charming pilot and ... and what? What was she exactly? She wasn't a schoolgirl even though she felt as worldly-wise as one. No, she was a homeless, rootless shadow who didn't know where she was heading.

Eventually, Luke fell silent. Samira stared out of the windscreen with unseeing eyes; she couldn't bear to look at Luke now. He had a smear of the ruby, red lipstick which Vera had been wearing on his cheek and she could now detect a floral fragrance that hadn't been in the car before.

"We've just passed Brentwood, it won't be long now," he said as they stopped at a T-junction and turned right.

"Thank you." She sighed. He must think her so dull. If the journey was now dragging for her, how much more must he be longing to reach Joanna's house in Laindon?

He gently cleared his throat. "You know, it's all right to feel upset, Samira."

She looked at him in alarm, "Upset?" The colour drained from her face. Surely, she couldn't be so transparent that he knew what she'd been thinking?

"Yes, it must be hard to uproot and start again after you've lost your grandmother. But you'll love Joanna. I promise. She'll make you feel at home in no time. And I'm sure you'll be good friends with Lexie – everyone loves her. She's great fun."

Samira let out the breath she'd been holding.

"Yes, I suppose so. Thank you." Thank goodness, he'd misread her silence.

"I hope you don't mind," he said, "but I'd like to ask a favour."

"Yes?" Samira looked at him in surprise. What on earth could she do for him?

"It's Lexie. I love her completely, but she's rather … well … head-strong. She acts before she thinks, and I wondered if you'd look out for her while I'm not around. You seem very sensible and level-headed, and I know you'll be a good influence on her … if you don't mind that is …"

So that's what he thought of her. 'Sensible and level-headed'. More like 'boring and dull'. *Well, it could be worse, at least it hadn't been 'silly and childish'.*

"Yes, of course," she said wondering what Lexie would think about his request.

Samira looked out across the fields. They stretched as far as she could see, and she longed for the journey to end. Surely it couldn't be much further. Suddenly, the peace of the countryside was broken as an air raid siren began to wail.

Luke accelerated, gripping the steering wheel tightly.

"We need to find somewhere to shelter," he said leaning forward and taking in the sky at the same time as he concentrated on the road. "I know it looks pretty quiet here in the country, but it's not called Bomb Alley for nothing. The Germans fly over here and up the Thames corridor to London and it's not unknown for them to drop the bombs they still have onboard on the way home."

Further ahead, where the lane bent sharply to the right, a collection of roofs could be seen above tall hedges, suggesting the presence of a farm. Far up in the sky, but approaching them rapidly was what looked like a swarm of bees.

"We'll shelter wherever the farmer is," Luke said and swung the car up to the house. He groaned when he saw the door and windows of the farmhouse had been boarded up. The wheels spun, flinging up dust, as Luke rapidly reversed the car and drove towards the barn on the other side of the large farmyard. The drone of aeroplanes now could be heard above the roar of the car's motor.

"As soon as I open the doors, run into the barn. I'll drive the car in if there's enough room." Luke leapt out of the driver's seat. He ran to the doors, flung them wide open, to reveal a dark, cavernous interior.

"Come on!" he shouted, beckoning to her, but instead of getting out of the car, Samira had already slipped into the driver's seat and taking off the handbrake, she slowly edged the car forward.

The interior of the barn was dark, although here and there cracks in the wooden planks of the walls allowed thin shafts of light to penetrate the gloom. Rusty chains hung from the rafters at one end of the building over an ancient tractor, assorted engines and a heap of tools. Samira had no idea how to turn the headlights on, so she eased the car into the darkness slowly, hoping there was nothing in her path until she was clear of the doors, then she stopped and turned off the engine. In the rear-view mirror, she saw Luke look up to check the progress of the enemy planes, then firmly close the door.

"Well, I wasn't expecting that!" Luke said with admiration as he opened the driver's door and helped her out.

"I learned to drive in the WVS," she said shyly, aware he was still holding her hand. When she'd imagined how that might feel several hours ago, she hadn't envisaged they'd be sheltering from enemy aeroplanes in the seclusion of a deserted barn. Luke put his other arm protectively around her shoulders and they stood together, allowing their eyes to become accustomed to the ribbon-striped darkness, listening to the throb of the engines as the aeroplanes passed overhead.

"You're shaking," he said, "don't worry, they're heading to London and I'm sure they won't waste a bomb on an old barn. We're probably only in danger when they're on their way home. We'll be fine, I'm sure."

How could she tell him she'd faced worse threats in London? She was trembling because he was holding her close. How could this man have such an effect on her? Of course, he could never be hers, but it didn't stop her body from responding to his touch.

Was it so wrong to pretend they belonged together – just for a short time? With bombers flying above – it was unlikely but possible – this could be their final moments, so who would it harm if she dreamed?

He pulled her close, turning her towards him, and holding her head against his chest, he gently stroking her hair. Waves of pleasure rippled throughout her body at his touch.

A rat scampered across the floor and dived under the old tractor, causing a small avalanche of tools, making them jump.

"We might as well make ourselves comfortable, we could be here for a while," said Luke, letting her go. He found a travel rug on the back seat of the car, and folding it up, he placed it on a large wooden beam.

"I know it's not very comfortable but if there's an emergency, we'll be able to escape faster from here than we would if we were sitting in the car."

The seat was only wide enough for them both if Luke put his arm around her and they squeezed together.

"Tell me more about India," he said, leaning his head against hers.

She knew he was trying to distract her from the drone of the aircraft passing overhead and she tried to think of something interesting to tell him, but her mind was numb. The delicate scent of something filled her nostrils – was it sandalwood? It was hard to concentrate with him so close. When he spoke, his breath feather-brushed her cheek, sending a cascade of delight through her body.

Her mind seemed to have divided into two. One tiny part allowed her to tell Luke about her childhood in India, but the rest was given up to the pleasure of the pressure of his body against hers and the touch of his fingertips on her hair and cheek.

The shafts of light that filtered through the cracks in the walls were much softer than they'd been when she and Luke had first arrived and when the all-clear siren sounded, Samira judged it was late afternoon. Usually, the familiar wail was a welcome relief but now, even before Luke moved away from her, the heat between their bodies cooled. The roar of the planes had long since faded into the distance but neither of them had remarked on it. Now, with the siren, there was no ignoring they must resume their journey.

He stood and, taking her hands, raised her up.

"Well, we survived," he said, brushing down his uniform. "Now I suppose we ought to hurry up and get to Priory Hall. Joanna and Lexie will be frantic with worry. I'll open the barn doors. D'you think you'll be able to reverse out?"

She nodded, too disappointed to speak. *How wonderful it would have been to have remained together a while longer.* But of course, they couldn't have stayed there any longer. That had been fairy tale. This was real life. Samira reversed into the farmyard, then slid over to the passenger seat. Luke got into the car and as she caught sight of the lipstick smear on his cheek, her stomach sank. It had been too dark to see it in the barn and she'd forgotten about it – and about Vera. While they'd been sitting together on the tartan rug, Samira hadn't been able to smell the floral fragrance that had clung to Luke as tightly as Vera had clung to him at Archie's house, but now, it filled the car – sweet and sickly.

"You might want to clean your cheek," she said offering him a handkerchief. He glanced in the mirror and winced.

"Vera," he said and wiped the mark away, "I don't know why she wears all that stuff on her face. She's good-looking enough without it. Anyway, thanks for telling me and I'll get this washed for you," he said tucking the handkerchief in his pocket.

"That's all right," said Samira, "I thought it best you didn't turn up at Joanna's house covered in lipstick. And don't worry about the handkerchief."

She didn't want it back. It was now tainted.

Lexie was waiting at the gates to Priory Hall when they arrived, and she ran towards them.

"Thank goodness you're both all right! I was so worried when the air raid siren went off. I wondered if you'd be in the middle of nowhere and wouldn't find anywhere to shelter. I couldn't bear to lose my baby brother and my new best friend to be."

"Baby brother! You're only a few minutes older than me, Lex. Come on, hop in, I'll give you a lift up the drive."

When they stopped outside the house, Joanna opened the door with a small boy in her arms and a girl at her side.

"I'm so glad you're both safe," she said. "Come in. Samira, this is Mark." She turned so they could see the young boy's face, but he buried it in his mother's neck.

"Poor boy. He's still not over his earache," Joanna whispered. "He isn't usually as quiet as this, is he, Faye?" she asked the girl who was peering up at Samira with undisguised admiration.

"Are you really an Indian princess?" Faye asked.

Samira crouched. "Well, I'm half-Indian but I'm sorry to disappoint you – I'm afraid I'm not a princess."

"But you're beautiful like a princess," Faye said, "and your hair's shiny, just like satin. Could you make mine look like that?"

"Your hair is lovely as it is," said Samira touching one of the brown curls that had escaped from the clip that restrained the rest of her hair.

"Shall we let Samira settle in before we plague her for hairdressing tips?" Joanna smiled. "I'm going to take this little man back to bed and then we'll have dinner. Ben's gone to fetch his mother. She's living in our house in Dunton at the moment, although I have a feeling she'll soon be moving back in with us. But let's get your things and take you to your room, Samira."

Lexie took Samira's arm and with Faye skipping ahead and Luke following with Samira's cases, they went upstairs.

"I hope you don't mind sharing with me," said Lexie. "We could have had a bedroom each but Mrs Richardson – that's Ben's mother, not Joanna, although of course, she's Mrs Richardson as well although I wouldn't dream of calling her that, because she told me to call her Joanna …" Lexie took a breath. "Anyway, the Old Mrs Richardson will probably be living here from now on. She moved into the cottage because she was finding the stairs difficult, but she's had several falls recently and since she lives alone, everyone thinks it's better if she comes here." She turned to Faye, "Would you be a love and fetch Samira a clean towel please, Faye?"

Lexie checked that Faye had gone, and lowered her voice. "Not that Mrs Richardson's happy about coming here. Apparently, she doesn't like Joanna – never has – and I think she's going to be quite a handful. Trust me, there are going to be fireworks."

"How could anyone not like Joanna?" Samira asked.

"What's that about not liking Joanna?" asked Luke who'd just appeared at the bedroom door with Samira's cases.

"We're talking about Old Mrs Richardson," said Lexie. "Ben's family are very well-to-do and when Joanna first came to Dunton, she was almost penniless. Her mother had left her the deeds to a plot on Dunton Plotlands and Joanna thought there'd be a cottage on it but when she got here, she found it was just a piece of land – no house, nothing – and she had no money to build one." Lexie took a deep breath. "So, the neighbours took her in, and she got a job at Ben's firm Richardson, Bailey & Cole, and ... well, they fell in love. It was so romantic! But Mrs Richardson didn't think Joanna was good enough for her son – and by all accounts, she still doesn't—"

Luke cleared his throat, heralding the return of Faye carrying a pile of towels.

"I didn't know which one to bring, so I brought them all," she said, peeping shyly around the heap.

Samira unpacked and Lexie helped her put everything away, while telling her about life at Priory Hall.

"Ben's really a solicitor. When his father died, he became a partner in Richardson, Bailey & Cole but now, with the war on, he's using the estate to grow food. That's why he hasn't been called up. Not that he wouldn't like to go. And Joanna's terrified he might yet join up. But so far, he's managing the estate with some farmworkers and a few Land Army girls. I've been helping them. The weather's been lovely, and I'm used to farm work, so I've been teaching them how to milk cows and other things. They all come from London, so they haven't much idea about farming. And then, of course, there's the Italians."

Lexie was lying face down on her bed, resting on her elbows, with knees bent and feet waving in the air.

"Italians?"

"Yes, you know, the men who were living in Britain before the outbreak of war and who've now been interned. We've got half a dozen working on the farm."

Samira looked at Lexie. The tone of her voice had changed when she'd spoken about the Italians – it had become soft and dreamy. But Lexie's face was turned away and Samira wondered if she'd just imagined it. Perhaps Lexie didn't like the injustice of men who'd lived in Britain for years being removed from their families and held in camps.

Lexie got off the bed and looked out of the window.

"Do you have any plans while you're here, Samira?" she asked.

"No. I want to do my bit for the war effort, but I thought I'd wait until I settled in before I decided."

"Then you must come and work with the Land Girls and me."

"And the Italians?" Samira smiled.

Lexie turned away but Samira thought she saw her face reddened. "Well, yes, I suppose so," she said, and then added quickly. "Anyway, I can see Ben's car turning into the drive. Come on, let's go down and help Joanna. I don't suppose Mrs Richardson is going to make this evening easy for her."

Lexie was correct.

"It's like being hauled up before the headmaster, knowing you're going to get a caning," whispered Luke as he stood with Joanna, Lexie and Samira in the hall. They were waiting to greet Mrs Richardson on her arrival at Priory Hall.

"Shhh!" said Lexie, elbowing him. "Behave!"

He'd described the mood quite accurately, thought Samira, who, despite never having met Ben's mother, had the sinking feeling she'd always experienced whenever she'd waited outside Sister Mary Benedicta's office.

The crunch of the tyres on the drive told them Ben and his mother had arrived, and Joanna closed her eyes, fixed a smile on her face. Stepping forward, she opened the door.

Samira was surprised to see a tiny, bird-like woman leaning heavily on Ben's arm as they slowly climbed the steps into the house. From Lexie's description, she'd imagined someone much larger and more aggressive looking. It didn't seem as if this woman would be able to withstand a puff of wind.

Ben handed his mother over to Joanna and excused himself while he fetched her bags from the car.

"Benjamin!" Mrs Richardson's voice was much stronger than Samira was expecting from her frail appearance. "Since when have you carried bags about? Send a servant!" She glared at Joanna as if it was her fault Ben had forgotten his heritage.

"I've been carrying bags about, mother, since the last servant left," he said quietly. "There's a war on. People are no longer fetching and carrying for the elite few, they're sacrificing themselves fighting for our freedom."

"Really. Then who are these?" She waved her arm at Samira, Lexie and Luke.

"Several of Joanna's relatives who've come to stay."

Mrs Richardson sniffed and looked the three young people up and down.

"And what about the foreigner?" She pointed at Samira. "Is she staying in the house?"

There was a sharp intake of breath, with eyes swivelling left and right to see who was going to react.

Ben was the first to speak. "This is Samira and she's one of Joanna's second cousins. She is very welcome in this house. She is a guest. As are you. And any guest in my house is treated with respect."

Mrs Richardson sniffed and peered at Samira. "A bit on the dark side but pretty enough, I suppose." Then turning back to Ben, she added, "but some of us still know how to maintain standards, Benjamin. I have a servant even though I live in that tiny, miserable house."

"That tiny, miserable house you mention, mother, was the house I built on Plotlands, and no one is forcing you to live there. You left this house voluntarily because you told us you couldn't manage the stairs. Joanna and I pay the girl who cooks and cleans for you double the going rate in order to keep her. She's just handed her notice in as she's now old enough to join up, so you no longer have a servant. They are things of the past for most people now."

"I see. Well, all I can say is, what a sorry state of affairs. Where's my walking stick?" She let go of Joanna's arm and hobbled into the dining room.

Joanna took Ben's arm and squeezed it, as he shook his head in dismay and disbelief.

*I'm sorry,* he mouthed to Lexie, Luke and Samira.

"Don't worry, it's not your fault," whispered Luke, and then said more loudly. "But I'd like to say she was wrong about one thing. Samira isn't pretty – she's absolutely beautiful."

And linking his arm through Samira's, he led her into the dining room.

"Thank you," she whispered. His quick wit, had helped to lighten the situation – even if he didn't mean it.

Surprisingly, the meal wasn't a disaster despite Mrs Richardson's initial behaviour. Perhaps she realised it would be far more pleasant for everyone if she were civil, and at the end of the meal, she even grudgingly complimented Joanna's cooking. Luke entertained them with stories about his fellow pilots and their antics and if he hadn't talked about Archie so much, Samira would have felt completely at ease. But the mention of Archie brought back memories of his sister, Vera, with her confidence and glamorous looks.

She glanced at Lexie, taking in her clothes and hairstyle, then looked down at her dress – the same one she'd worn to Gran's funeral – and she determined to ask Lexie to help her. She could easily blame rationing for her lack of style but everyone else seemed to manage. Even Joanna, with two children and an enormous house, seemed to find time to look elegant with her chestnut curls caught back off her face and her smart dress.

By the end of the meal, Samira was feeling so shabby that when Ben said he'd help Joanna clear away and suggested Lexie and Luke show her around the garden, she almost made excuses and escaped to her bedroom.

"Come on, Samira, you'll love it," Luke said. "The sunset's going to be glorious this evening."

How could she refuse?

Once they were out of sight of the dining room, Lexie said she was going to the Land Army girls' cottage to discuss the following day's work and left Samira and Luke at the lake.

"She wasn't so keen on farming when we were in Devon," said Luke, "but I suppose she wants to do her bit for the war effort. I can't blame her for that. She tells me you're going to help on the farm too."

"Yes, although I've never worked on the land before. When I was young, I used to watch the women in the plantation picking the young leaves off the tea bushes but other than sowing a few seeds in Gran's backyard – which never grew – that's my entire experience."

"I'm sure everyone will help you until you know what you're doing. Anyway, you might find your driving skills mean you're in demand to drive the tractor."

"Yes, I hadn't thought of that. It's funny, not so long ago, Sister Mary Benedicta asked me what I was going to do when I left school. Driving a tractor wasn't something that crossed my mind."

"Becoming a pilot's always been my dream but I never really believed it'd come true. And in two days' time, I'll be flying my own plane across the Channel." He sighed. "Well, let's not think about tomorrow. Let's go and watch the sun go down. You never know how many more you'll see." He laughed but Samira could hear an edge to his voice and knew it had been bravado.

"Come on," he said, taking her hand and leading her up the slope along a narrow path between dense bushes. When they reached the top, the undergrowth gave way to lush grass and the ground fell away steeply.

"This is the best place to see the sunset," he said.

Samira wondered how he knew. But she dared not ask who he'd shared the spectacle with before.

Perhaps it had been Lexie.

*Perhaps it had been Vera,* her inner voice whispered.

"Shall we sit down?" he asked. "I wish I'd thought to bring something to sit on. Here, let's use this." He started to take his jacket off.

"That's fine, it's quite dry." She sat on the grass.

He looked at her for a second and joined her. "You know, you're so easy to be with. Most girls would complain about grass stains on their dresses and goodness knows what. But you ... you're so natural and ... well, easy to be with."

He put his jacket around her shoulders and held it in place with his arm.

Pale orange and pink tinged the dilute blue of the sky. The underside of the fluffy clouds that drifted above the woods on the horizon, glowed yellow, then orange. Eventually, the brilliant disc slipped behind the trees leaving a rosy blush.

Despite Luke's jacket, Samira shivered. But it wasn't simply the chill of the evening breeze now the sun had set. She'd seen tropical sunsets in India with skies the colour of jewels. They made this appear quite insipid, but she'd never been as moved as she felt now, watching this Essex sundown with Luke's arm around her shoulders and the warmth of his body against hers.

The last hint of pink faded in the sky as the blue deepened, and here and there, stars began to flicker.

"We'd better go back." Luke rose, and extending his hand to help Samira up, he pulled her close and wrapped his arms around her.

"I wish I had more time to be with you," he said. "I've only spent one day with you, and yet it feels like I've known you for a long time ..." He sighed. "I can't promise you anything ..." He ran his hand through his hair. "I don't even know if I'll be alive by the end of the week ... but it would mean so much to me if I knew you'd be here for me ..."

"Yes," she whispered. "When will you be back?"

He gently shook his head and placed a finger on her lips then he closed his eyes and leant towards her. She held her breath and waited for his lips to replace his finger.

"Luke! Samira!" It was Lexie.

Luke let go of Samira and stepped back guiltily.

"We're here," he called.

Lexie emerged from the bushes and despite the growing darkness, Samira saw she was frowning.

"Oh, there you are." She scowled at them. "The sun went down ages ago. Don't you think we ought to go back?"

"Lexie?" Luke said gently.

But she'd already turned back into the bushes and was gone.

Luke held out his hand to Samira and they walked back silently holding hands until they were within sight of the house.

Then Luke let go of her hand.

# Chapter Eleven

L exie was in bed when Samira entered their bedroom. She'd left the bedside lamp alight on the chest of drawers between their two beds, but she lay rigid and motionless, her face turned to the wall. Samira undressed quietly. It seemed her friendship with Lexie was over before it had even begun. How the day could have finished like this, Samira had no idea, but she was certain she couldn't stay in Priory Hall now, sharing a room, and her life, with a girl she'd unintentionally upset.

Tomorrow, she'd look for a way of getting back to India. Ships still sailed from England to other parts of the world, and yes, there might be a threat of being torpedoed by the Germans, but it was a risk she was willing to take to get to somewhere she might be able to call home. And it wasn't like she was completely safe here. Hadn't Luke described this area as 'Bomb Alley'?

She'd walk into Laindon in the morning and find out if she could book a ticket on a ship with the money Gran had left her. Papa wouldn't be happy, having told Pop not to let her return, but by the time anyone realised she'd gone, it would be too late to do anything about it. Lexie would be getting up at four o'clock to help with the milking, Luke was returning to the RAF base at Hornchurch and with

Mrs Richardson moving back into the house, Joanna would be busy – so no one would miss her. It would have been nice to know what she'd done to make Lexie so annoyed, though.

She sighed and reached out to turn off the bedside lamp.

"Oh, it's no good, Sam," said Lexie. "I can't sleep when I feel guilty."

"Guilty?"

"I upset you, and I upset Luke, and now I feel dreadful." Lexie sighed. She sat up, rested her chin on her knees and hugged her legs.

"I expect Luke'll be cross with me," she added, "but then, I'm very cross with him."

"You are?" Well, this wasn't what Samira had expected at all.

"Yes, and I've got every right to be angry." Lexie's eyes blazed. "He promised." She sighed again. "But on the other hand, I was in a bad mood because ... well ... that's another story. And of course, that wasn't his fault at all ... And it certainly wasn't *your* fault. To think you got caught up in all that. What must you think of us?"

"I honestly don't know," said Samira. "But I think I must have done something—"

"Darling! You didn't do anything. Trust me. Luke simply has no idea how devastatingly handsome he is. Back in Devon, most of the girls in the village were in love with him but he just wasn't interested. He broke a string of hearts. Girls just don't seem to be able to resist him. The trouble is, he doesn't mean to, but he can easily ... well ... lead a girl on."

"But he didn't do anything ..."

"No, I know. But he promised me he'd be more careful. Especially now he's joined the RAF. And he agreed. He promised! He said he'd just have fun, but he wouldn't let anything go further than that. Not until the war's over, at any rate."

"Fun?" The word stabbed at Samira like a knife. Did Lexie believe Luke had just been having fun with her?

"Well, yes. He's a pilot, not a monk. I know that, and I know those boys face death each time they fly, so they must have some sort of recreation, but I've told Luke it's not fair to lead anyone on and give the impression he's serious. Now he's a pilot, his life expectancy's measured in weeks. He knows he's got nothing to offer a girl. He won't even tell anyone when his next leave is because he thinks it's unlucky."

Samira remembered him holding his finger to her lips when she'd asked him when he'd be back. So, it had all been a bit of fun? A way of amusing himself before he returned to Hornchurch.

"Well, I suppose we should be grateful you've hardly had any time to get to know him, and I put a stop to things before they had a chance to get serious," said Lexie. "I may well have saved you a lot of heartache, Samira. I hope you don't mind me making assumptions about you but if you've spent much of your life in a convent, I don't suppose you're very experienced with men …"

Samira blushed. "Well … No, I suppose not. But you don't need to worry about me, Luke really isn't my type."

Lexie looked at her with a quizzical expression. "Well, if you're sure …"

"Oh yes. Definitely." Samira pushed the words past the lump in her throat and forced her lips into a smile. "Anyway, perhaps we'd better get some sleep. We've got to be up early tomorrow." Then before Lexie could see the tears in her eyes, she turned the light out.

Lexie swung her legs off the bed. "I'm so glad we sorted that out. I couldn't have slept a wink with that on my mind. I think I'll go and apologise to Luke now. I couldn't bear it if he left in the morning before I had a chance to make up. I'd never forgive myself if …" The end of the sentence hung in the air between them.

She tiptoed to the door.

"I won't be long. I'll try not to wake you when I come back. Night, night."

"Night, night." Samira hoped Lexie hadn't heard her voice break. Hot, bitter tears rolled down her cheeks. It wouldn't matter how much noise Lexie made when she came back, Samira would not be asleep.

How could she have been so stupid? She'd seen Luke with Vera earlier that day.

Earlier that day?

Had it only been a few hours before that she'd left Stepney with Luke? So much had happened. Lexie had read her correctly; other than Jimmy, she'd had very little experience with men. And today, she'd surpassed herself. She'd been about to fall in love with a man whose sister admitted he was a heartbreaker.

Considering the hour, Lexie was remarkably cheerful. She turned the alarm clock off seconds after it rang at four o'clock as if she'd been waiting for it. Samira, on the other hand, had lain awake for hours and when she'd finally fallen asleep, her dreams had been filled with Luke. He'd walked away from her, and she'd run after him, calling repeatedly but he hadn't stopped, nor had he turned to look at her. She'd woken from her dreams, feeling exhausted.

"Darling! You look dreadful! Are you feeling all right? Your eyes are all red and puffy. If you're not well, stay in bed."

"No, I'm fine thanks." It wasn't true but a day at home wasn't going to solve her problems. The war would still be raging whether she was moping in bed or not, and the only sensible course of action was to carry on as if she'd never met Luke.

She'd heard him rev his motorbike shortly before Lexie's alarm had rung and then the crunch of the stones on the drive as he'd roared away.

Lexie lent Samira a pair of overalls and tied her hair up so it could be easily tucked into her hat. She hummed a tune as she brushed her own hair and arranged it in victory rolls, then dabbed cologne behind her ears. When she noticed Samira look at her with a puzzled expression, she blushed.

"Well," she said defensively. "Just because we're working on the land, doesn't mean we can't look our best."

A quick application of powder on her nose and a little lipstick finished her preparations and she led a weary, gritty-eyed Samira downstairs to breakfast.

Joanna was at the kitchen sink washing up, as they entered the kitchen.

"Morning," she said cheerily, "help yourselves to breakfast. Ben and Luke have already eaten and left. Oh, by the way, Ben said he'll see you after milking. He seemed to think you know where to go today."

"Oh yes," said Lexie cheerfully, "Is Mark better today?"

"Yes, thanks. Well, he slept all night, so I think he's almost back to normal. If Mother-in-Law's up to it, I'm hoping she'll play with him today, then Faye and I can get on with the vegetable garden. Are you all right, Samira?" she asked anxiously, "you're looking rather pale."

"Yes, I'm fine, thanks." Samira tipped her head down as she concentrated on slicing a loaf.

"As soon as I get a chance, we'll sit down together and have a talk about what you want to do in the future, then we'll see what we can do to make it happen – Herr Adolf Hitler willing, of course." She rolled her eyes to the ceiling and put her arm around Samira's shoulders. "But until you've made plans, I'm sure you'll miss everything that was once familiar. It's perfectly all right to feel bit homesick, you know."

"Thank you." Samira was touched by Joanna's thoughtfulness, but she couldn't have explained she wasn't homesick at all. That would have required her to be longing for somewhere she considered home.

"Ready?" Lexie asked as she drained the last of her tea and grabbed one of the slices of bread Samira had cut.

"Anyone would think you loved digging ditches, Lexie." said Joanna.

"No ditches today, Ben says we're going to cut hay. But we've got to milk the cows first. Are you ready, Sam?"

"Someone's happy," Joanna said as Lexie left the kitchen humming a tune.

The sun was beginning to brighten the sky to the east as Samira closed the front door. Lexie held two bicycles and she mounted one and held the other out.

Samira looked at it in horror. She'd never ridden a bicycle before but felt too foolish to admit it. It couldn't be so hard to ride, could it? She took it by the handlebars and copied Lexie who'd already begun to pedal down the drive. Her first attempt ended with her breaking her fall on the lawn and by the time she'd reached the gates of Priory Hall, she'd tumbled off twice and only managed to keep her feet on the pedals for a few seconds.

"Why didn't you tell me you couldn't ride a bicycle?" Lexie asked when Samira finally caught up with her. She'd given up trying to pedal and was now pushing it along by the handlebars.

"I felt too stupid."

"Darling! Don't worry! It's not that hard – look, I can do it, so it can't be difficult. We'll make time today to teach you. But you can't wheel it all the way to the milking shed. If you put one foot on the pedal and hold the handlebars, you can scoot along. It'll be faster."

Despite deep shadows obscuring ruts and potholes, Samira managed to propel the bike along, gradually finding it easier to balance – although she admitted to herself, there wasn't far to fall, and it would be very different when she mounted the saddle. But it was faster than walking and she hadn't lagged too far behind.

"You must be Samira," said the tallest of the Women's Land Army girls, when she and Lexie arrived. "I understand you're staying with the Richardsons. I'm Cissie and this is Marge." She indicated a smaller, plumper girl with mousy hair and freckles. Pointing to a third girl, she said, "And this is the new girl, Ruth who arrived yesterday morning. Ruth, this is Lexie and Samira."

"Pleased to meet you, ladies." Her accent gave her away as someone who might be more used to afternoon tea in the drawing room, than milking cows as the sun was rising.

"She won't last the week," whispered Marge.

"Shut up and give her a chance." Cissie nudged her, then added. "Rightio, girls, let's get cracking."

They finished the milking and were walking back to the Land Girls' cottage to make a cup of tea when it suddenly occurred to Samira how strange it was Lexie and the new girl, Ruth, had never met. The previous evening, when Luke had taken her to watch the sunset, Lexie had said she was going to see the Land Army girls, so why hadn't she met Ruth?

There could, of course, be many explanations. Ruth may have been tired after her journey and might have gone to bed before Lexie had called. But nothing that had happened that morning during milking suggested Lexie had seen Cissie or Marge the previous day either.

The girls had been incredulous when Samira admitted she'd never learned to ride a bicycle, but Lexie considerately pointed out a convent probably wasn't the best place to acquire skills like that. When they took a short cut across the fields to the cottage where the Land Girls were staying, Samira was relieved. The ground was too uneven to cycle across and she and Lexie wheeled their bicycles over the ruts.

"Slow down please, ladies, I've got a blister on my heel," said Ruth.

Marge rolled her eyes and nudged Cissie who ignored her.

"A nice, strong cuppa will sort that out," said Cissie. "And guess what? Mr Richardson dropped by last night. His wife sent over some bacon rashers, so it's bacon sandwiches all round this morning."

"Have we got time?" Lexie checked her watch.

"Time? There's always time for tea and a bacon sandwich," said Marge. "It's all right for you living up at the big house, I don't suppose you're ever hungry, but us working girls need our food. I haven't had bacon for ... well, I can't even remember. The last farmer I worked for was so mean, I think he fed his pigs better than his Land Girls."

"That's shocking," said Lexie.

"I know. He actually thought he was doing us a favour when he allowed us to dip our bread in the fat his bacon had been cooked in. What an absolute beast! He wasn't married, and he expected us to cook and clean as well as do the farm work. You'd have thought he'd have been grateful to have us and would've treated us well."

"I had a similar experience," said Cissie. "Except my farmer was married and it was his wife who treated us badly. Her two sons are away fighting, and I think she resented us taking their places on the farm. We tried to be sympathetic but ..." She paused and shrugged. "Still, war affects people in different ways and I've no idea what it must be like to have two sons in danger."

"Well, you're more generous and understanding than me," said Marge. "I'd have given her the sharp edge of my tongue!"

"I don't doubt it," said Cissie.

"I certainly put my farmer in his place before I walked out," said Marge. "Mind you, he got his own back. I'd been there six weeks before I gave him a piece of my mind and left, but he refused to pay me a penny."

"Well, let's be thankful Mr Richardson's a gentleman and so far, he's treated us well," said Cissie. "And Mrs Richardson of course. And as for those adorable children! Such darlings. All the prisoners love them too."

"Oh," said Samira with a smile. "For a second there, I thought you said *prisoners*."

"I did."

"Prisoners?"

"Yes," said Cissie. "We've got about six Germans and four Italians. I would've thought Lexie would have mentioned them."

Lexie blushed.

"Germans and Italians? Here?" asked Samira.

"Oh yes, it's just a small camp up the road and the inmates help out on Mr Richardson's farm."

"In fact, as soon as we've had tea, we'll be heading off to the hayfield and they'll be helping us," said Marge. "But don't worry," she added "they're all very civilised and friendly. Most of them speak passable English too."

"So, you mean to say we'll be helping the enemy?" Ruth was so incensed; she could barely speak. "That's outrageous!"

"No, don't be an idiot – they'll be helping us. There's a difference," said Cissie patiently. "And just remember, for every enemy POW on British soil, there's likely to be a British POW on enemy soil. If we look after theirs, we can only hope they'll look after ours."

"Well, I don't know about that!" Ruth sniffed. "I didn't join the Land Army to work alongside the enemy!"

"Just out of interest, what did you join it for?" Marge asked. "I would've thought you'd be more at home knitting socks in the comfort of an armchair."

"Well, you'd be wrong," said Ruth sharply. "I'm just as capable as you of doing my bit in the fresh air."

Marge snorted. "Well, let's see if you still feel the same after a day in the hayfield."

"So, which cottage is yours?" asked Samira trying to change the subject. If she hadn't remarked on the prisoners, the conversation wouldn't have taken such a turn.

Peace-loving Cissie was happy to answer and steer Ruth and Marge away from an argument. "We're in the one on the left. Next to us is Bill Grant, or 'Grunt', as we call him, and then the two next to him are empty – they used to house farmhands, but they've all joined up. Old Grunt's too old to fight, so he's still here helping Mr Richardson, although he's not in favour of having us on the farm."

The mention of Bill Grant united the girls once more.

"What a terribly rude man!" said Ruth. "He came out of his cottage when I arrived and waved his stick at me. Well, how was I to know I'd knocked on the wrong door?"

"Did he indeed?" said Marge in a menacing voice. "Just let me see him do that again and I'll really let him have it."

Cissie smiled as she linked arms with the two other Land Army girls and walked up the path to the cottage door.

Ruth went upstairs and appeared a few minutes later with a rose-patterned china cup and saucer. "I prefer my tea in a proper cup." She held it out to be filled from the large teapot Cissie was holding.

Turning bacon slices over in the frying pan at the stove, Marge rolled her eyes but said nothing.

They crowded around the small kitchen table that Ruth insisted on washing down twice, and Marge served up bacon between thick slices of bread.

"Mmm, that was delicious." Cissie, wiped her mouth. "If you're not going to eat that, Lexie, I'll have it," she said pointing to Lexie's plate.

"I'm going to take it with me for later," Lexie said and blushed.

Samira saw Marge and Cissie frown and exchange worried looks.

Cissie placed her hand on Lexie's shoulder. "You're heading for trouble, you know," she said kindly.

"I don't know what you mean!" Lexie shook her hand off. "I don't have to eat this now."

"Have it your own way," said Cissie.

Samira was desperate to ask what was going on but fearful of inadvertently starting an argument like she'd almost done before between Ruth and Marge. She had a feeling it wouldn't be long before she found out.

Ruth insisted everything was washed up and put away before they left. "Well, I don't want to come back to a mess, even if you do," she said.

"Trust me," said Marge, "by the time we've dealt with all that hay and got home, you won't care if your precious cup and saucer are dirty or not."

"So, shall we go?" asked Lexie, wrapping her sandwich in a clean handkerchief and putting it in her pocket.

"I thought you were a farm girl," said Cissie, "you know we've got to wait till the dew's burnt off the hay before we start."

"I know that," said Lexie. "But we've still got to get there."

"It only takes five minutes across the fields. We'll just be standing around if we go now."

By the time Ruth had finished the washing up, Cissie decided it was time to leave and Lexie rushed outside, followed by Marge and Ruth. Cissie placed a restraining hand on Samira's arm.

"You're going to have to keep an eye on your friend," she said.

"Why? What's going on?"

"You'll find out soon enough."

Cissie was right. Samira soon realised why Lexie had been so keen to get to the hayfield. Other small clues she hadn't noticed or understood before, suddenly made sense – the cheerfulness at getting up at four o'clock in the morning, the humming, the perfume, powder and lipstick, and the blushing at the mention of the Italians. And of course, the bacon sandwich that Samira saw pass covertly from Lexie's hands to those of one of the men.

She knew they were prisoners because each man had a large, circular, red patch sewn to the front of one trouser leg and on the back of his jacket, so they could easily be distinguished from the civilian population. And if there had been any doubt, nearby stood an armed soldier.

Despite the circumstances, everyone seemed remarkably relaxed except Ruth, who stood apart from the others, watching.

"I don't like this," she whispered to Samira. "There are ten of them and only four women and one soldier. And they've all got pitchforks. By the time that dozy soldier picks his gun up and gets ready to defend us, we'll all be dead!"

"I don't think it's quite as drastic as that," said Samira. "All the prisoners seem very polite and Cissie and the other girls have worked with them before. If they thought there was a threat, they wouldn't be chatting to them like that, would they? And apparently, Joanna will be over later with Faye and Mark to bring some food. She wouldn't put her children in jeopardy."

"No, I suppose not. It just seems so contrary to everything I've ever thought. Our men are out in France being killed by men like this and here we are fraternising."

"These men are helping to feed Britain. Would it make our days any happier if we were nasty to them or simply ignored them? I think it's a very civilised way to behave and if I had a son who was a prisoner abroad, I'd want to know that he was being treated like this."

"Yes, I can see the sense in that. But I'm not sure I'd be flirting like Lexie is with one of them."

Samira remained silent. What was Lexie thinking? True, the Italian she was talking to was gorgeous and charming, but even Samira with her lack of experience could see this was not likely to end well for her.

"What a shame one of us couldn't drive the tractor," said Cissie. "We could do with all the men working on the ground. It's a waste having one of them in the tractor."

"I might be able to do it." When Samira saw Cissie's look of disbelief, she wished she hadn't. "I can drive a car and a van," she added defensively. "Is it much harder to drive a tractor?"

"No idea," said Cissie. "I suppose you could give it a go. What have we got to lose?" She smiled and slapped Samira on the back. "Well, I'll be blowed! You're a dark horse. You can't ride a bicycle, but you can drive a car!"

After a brief lesson from the German, Samira mastered the tractor and moved it forward as required so the others could toss the hay into the trailer and gradually, the field was cleared.

By the time Joanna arrived with Faye, much of the hay had been transferred to the barn. One of the prisoners crouched when he saw Faye and opened his arms wide. She flew into them and as he picked her up and swung her around, she squealed with delight.

"Poor man," remarked Joanna as she opened the car boot to get the trestle table. "He showed me a photo of his little girl and she looks a lot like Faye. He told me he misses her so much."

Ruth sidled up to Samira. "Well, I don't often admit I'm wrong, but it seems I was too quick to have judged the prisoners. If they didn't have accents and large, red dots on their uniforms, I don't think I'd know they were foreign. They've worked really hard today and despite being stuck here, they seem to be polite and good-natured. I'm still not sure it's a good idea to get quite so close to them though." She stared at Lexie.

"Oh, Riccardo, that's such a lot of nonsense!" Lexie said as the handsome Italian bent over her hand as if telling her fortune.

"Si, si, Lexie," he said. "Trust me. You will meet a tall, dark, 'and-some stranger." He pretended to point out the lines on her palm that were foretelling the event and then raised it to his lips and kissed it.

Samira glanced at Joanna who was getting jugs of drink and baskets of food out of the car. She was so busy arranging them on a trestle table, she didn't notice Lexie's palm reading.

Would Joanna be upset if she knew Lexie was keen on one of the Italians? Samira began to wonder if it was such a terrible thing. She remembered Mrs Thomsett saying the war was making people act rashly. So many doing things they wouldn't have done in peacetime because life was now so precarious, it seemed sensible to live for the day.

Luke had asked her to keep an eye on his sister because he knew she could be reckless, but Lexie just seemed to be having fun. What could she do with a man who spent his days in a field with a group of prisoners and a guard, and his nights locked up?

One of the Germans smiled at her. "Fräulein, do you know where is the young boy, Mark? I have a gift for him. I make it myself." He took a small carved aeroplane from his pocket and held it on the palm of his hand.

"He hasn't been very well," said Samira. "Shall I take it for him, or would you like to wait until he's better?"

"You will take it?" He put it in her hand. "You will tell him Karl made it for him, please?"

Samira assured him she would. She looked at the skilfully carved plane and thought of Luke. Her stomach lurched when she remembered how much danger he was now facing as a pilot officer.

Angry tears came to her eyes. So many deaths, so much misery and yet, people who were supposed to be enemies could get on very well indeed, as shown by the day's events.

Karl spotted the tears in her eyes. "So much sadness in the world," he said, echoing her thoughts.

Samira planned to ask Lexie about Riccardo, but after the dinner table had been cleared, Lexie announced she was tired and went straight to their bedroom. It was probably just as well. Samira was exhausted too after their long, demanding day and the lack of sleep the previous night. And she didn't want to risk upsetting Lexie. Anyway, she decided, as she climbed into bed, what right did she have to comment? As Lexie had pointed out only yesterday, she had very little experience with men. So, what would she know?

During the following weeks, there was little free time to consider anything other than rising early, working in the fields, and going to bed straight after dinner. Gradually, Samira became accustomed to the long hours and the strenuous work and had even learned to ride her bicycle. It no longer alarmed her Lexie made her feelings for the good-looking Riccardo so obvious. It brightened Lexie's day when he was there, so what harm could there be in it?

One morning in early August, however, she wondered whether she ought to have talked to Lexie. After all, hadn't she promised Luke she'd look out for his sister?

# Chapter Twelve

T he sun had already risen when she awoke, and her eyelids felt swollen and heavy. Had Lexie's alarm failed to go off?

It was just after six o'clock – two hours after the alarm should have rung.

"Lexie! Wake up, the alarm didn't go off! We're late!"

But there was no reply.

Samira leapt up. Lexie's bed was neatly made as if it hadn't been slept in, but she'd definitely gone to bed at the same time as Samira the previous evening.

Samira quickly washed and dressed, then hurried down to the kitchen where Joanna, who was eating breakfast with Faye and Mark, looked up in surprise.

"I thought you and Lexie had already left for the day. Is everything all right?"

"Yes, thanks. I think I went back to sleep," Samira lied.

"I bet Lexie's wondering where you are."

"Yes, I expect so." Samira was certainly wondering where Lexie was.

She took a slice of bread and rushed out to fetch her bicycle, planning to ride to the Land Girls' cottage and see if Lexie was there. Her disappearance almost certainly had something to do with Riccardo but for the last few days, she and Lexie had been cleaning Joanna's house in Dunton Plotlands, so they hadn't seen the Land Girls or the POWs. Ben's mother had finally moved out of the small house and gone to stay with her sister; Joanna wanted it cleaned, ready for Ben's cousins whose house in London had been bombed. Samira had never seen Lexie so miserable.

Could she have crept out very early that morning to spend time with Riccardo? And if so, where could they have gone? Samira knew security wasn't tight in the prisoner of war camp – there was no need. The men weren't going to escape. The distinctive red patches on their clothes ensured they'd be easily spotted, and it was unlikely any of them could get to the coast and gain passage on a boat without being challenged. So long as the POWs were well-behaved, they had plenty of freedom.

Samira suddenly gasped as she realised where Lexie might take Riccardo, if she had indeed gone to find him. The obvious place was Joanna's Plotlands cottage.

The sky was clear, but mist still lingered, clinging to the ground. Samira shivered despite her jacket. As she rode along the drive, the cool air began to clear her bleary brain and she wondered if she'd jumped to the wrong conclusion. Perhaps it was simply that Lexie had woken early and not wanting to disturb her, had got ready and gone to help the Land Girls with the milking. Yes, that was surely the explanation. She was over-reacting.

Samira stopped at the end of the drive. She'd planned to go left and cycle to Joanna's house but now, she turned the handlebars to the right to head towards the Land Girls' cottage. The roar of an engine cut into her thoughts, and she hesitated, looking up fearfully in case there was an aeroplane approaching. But the sky was clear, and besides, she could now tell the sound was coming from her right. She paused to let the car – or whatever it was – go first before she pulled out on to the road. However, it wasn't a car, it was a motorbike, and it didn't pass the drive, it swung in and ground to a halt just behind her.

Her heart beat wildly in her chest when she realised it was Luke. He got off the bike and ran to meet her.

"Where're you off to on your own?" he asked, brushing his windswept fringe off his face. Since she'd last seen him, his hair had grown, his face was thinner and somehow, he seemed older – but of course, after the dangers he faced daily, that wasn't surprising.

"I'm looking for Lexie." The words were out before she had a chance to think. Now he'd wonder why she didn't know where his sister was.

"Well, she's not with the Land Girls. I've just met them. They said they hadn't seen her for a few days. I hear you've been cleaning the cottage in Plotlands."

She nodded, not sure what to say. How could she tell Luke her suspicions?

"D'you think she might be there?"

"Umm ..."

"Is there something wrong?"

"Well ..."

He looked at her for a few seconds, head on one side.

"Right, let's go and find out," he said walking back to the bike. "Come on, hop on behind me."

She straddled the bike and wrapped her arms around his middle as he revved the engine, pulled out of the drive, and accelerated along the road. The rush of wind took her breath away and she clung to Luke tightly, laying her cheek against his leather jacket while the hedgerows sped by so quickly, they were a blur. How enjoyable this ride would have been under other circumstances but now the dread they might find Lexie and Riccardo together at Joanna's house filled her mind.

Luke turned off on to the unmade road and slowed down. It was too uneven to go fast, and he wove his way through the furrows and ruts. As they drew up outside Joanna's house in Second Avenue, Samira could see Lexie's bike leaning against the veranda. Luke turned off the engine and in the silence which ensued, raised voices could be heard coming from the house.

Samira groaned softly. She couldn't hear what was being said but it sounded as though Lexie was pleading with an angry Riccardo.

"There's someone in there with Lexie," Luke said with surprise, then seeing Samira's anxious expression, he asked, "You know who it is?"

She nodded.

"Well, who is it?"

"Riccardo. I don't know his surname. He's one of the internees—"

Shock registered on his face.

"Please stay here," he said before rushing up the path, climbing the veranda steps and entering the house.

Samira was tempted to run around to the back of the house and peer in through the kitchen window, but she decided to respect Luke's wishes. This was, after all, a family matter. Lexie's screams and the crash of crockery cut through the early morning stillness of Second Avenue. Seconds later, a wild-eyed Riccardo appeared at the door. He looked right and left, then muttering in Italian, he pushed Samira out of the way and before she could react, he'd climbed on to Luke's motorbike. He started the ignition and drove off, bucking and bumping over the uneven road.

Samira ran up the steps and pushed open the door to find Lexie on her knees next to Luke who was lying motionless on his back surrounded by broken china.

"Sam! Thank goodness you're here! I don't know what to do. Luke's stopped breathing!"

# Chapter Thirteen

Samira's first aid training with the WVS took over and she knelt by Luke's side and took his pulse.

"He's breathing, but he needs attention. That gash over his eye looks nasty. I'll find something to staunch the flow but one of us needs to fetch help – and quickly."

"I'll go. Oh, Sam, thank goodness you're here. This is all my fault."

"Let's worry about that later," said Samira gently but firmly. "At the moment, we need help."

"Yes, yes, of course. I'll ride like the wind. I promise. Thank you, Sam." Lexie rushed out of the house to her bike.

Samira found Joanna's first aid box and cleaned all the cuts she could get to, without moving Luke. He was bleeding above one eye and as she dabbed at it with iodine, he groaned and stirred.

"Lie still," she said gently. "Lexie's gone for help. You're going to be fine."

"Samira?"

"I'm here."

"I can't see anything. It's all black."

"Try to relax. You've had a blow to the head. It might be the result of that. We'll soon have you in hospital. Don't worry."

"Where's that man? You're not in any danger, are you?"

"No. Don't worry about him, he's gone." She decided not to add to Luke's worries by telling him about the stolen motorbike. Riccardo would be picked up before long. The large, red patches on his leg and back would ensure he was recognised and stopped.

Luke glanced from side to side as if searching for something he could see. Was the sight loss temporary? How could that be? Ten minutes ago, he'd been steering a smooth path for them on his motorbike down a bumpy road, picking out every dip and mound on a journey she'd wanted to go on forever and now ...

She held his hand and whispered a fusion of wishes, thoughts and prayers – anything to try to reassure him, as his eyes sightlessly moved back and forth searching for the light.

The following day, Samira pedalled through the lane leading to the milking shed. It was earlier than normal because she hadn't been able to sleep, worrying about Luke and Lexie, so she'd finally decided to get up and do something useful. The Land Girls wouldn't be there for some time, but she could at least get ready for the day's milking and try to occupy her mind.

When Ben and Joanna had questioned her, she'd been able to tell them very little, although the fact that Lexie had been there with Riccardo had been damning enough. She didn't mention Lexie had said she blamed herself for what happened to Luke – they were just words spoken in the heat of the moment. Samira knew Ben and Joanna were angry, but neither of them were as critical of Lexie as she was of herself, so there was no point adding to her misery.

Cissie was the first to arrive, and she hugged Samira warmly.

"How's Lexie's brother? How's Lexie? What on earth happened yesterday? We haven't been able to talk about anything else."

Marge and Ruth appeared, both out of breath.

"I wish my legs were as long as yours, Cissie," said Marge gasping for breath, then she turned to Samira. "We hoped you'd come. We're desperate for news. Especially about Lexie's brother."

Samira admitted she didn't know a great deal except Lexie had stayed at the hospital overnight and that Luke's eyesight had improved slightly.

"So, Lexie was with Riccardo when you and Luke arrived?" Ruth asked.

Samira sighed and nodded.

"Well, that's a pretty poor show!" said Ruth.

"I know it wasn't wise," said Samira. "But she was head over heels in love with him. Love makes people do foolish things, doesn't it?"

"I'm not talking about Lexie," Ruth snapped. "I'm talking about that outrageous Italian prisoner. Fancy leading her on like that. I knew no good would come from working alongside the enemy."

"Oh, get off your high horse, Ruthie," said Cissie good-naturedly. "There's a war on. *Carpe diem* – seize the day."

"Yes, I'm perfectly aware of what *Carpe diem* means, thank you. But if you ask me, too many people are using that as an excuse to act like animals."

"No one was asking you," said Marge. "Lexie just fell in love. There's no law against it as far as I know."

"No, but it's not desirable when one party is married." Ruth crossed her arms over her chest.

There was silence for a few seconds.

Finally, Cissie said. "Riccardo was married?"

"Oh yes!" said Ruth hotly. "And he has a child."

"I didn't know!" said Cissie. "How do *you* know?"

"Karl told me. Apparently, Riccardo carries a photo of his family in his pocket. And he said he was desperate to get back to Italy to be with them."

"You've been getting very snugly with Karl, for someone who doesn't approve of fraternising with the enemy," said Marge.

"Oh, don't be ridiculous! Karl just has a similar taste to me in opera. That's all."

Samira looked at Ruth in horror. "So, you mean Riccardo was using Lexie?"

"It looks like it."

"Poor, poor Lexie. Her heart will be broken."

"Don't say it!" Cissie said to Ruth who'd opened her mouth to answer. "Don't say a word unless what you intend to say is kind."

Ruth closed her mouth.

Luke stared up at the lights suspended from the ward ceiling. At least he could see them now. The temporary blindness had frightened him, and he was enjoying all the sights that once he'd have taken for granted. If only he could see things sharply without it appearing everything was superimposed by a similar, but ghostly shape. His doctor had assured him that in time, the double vision would fade. But for now, he wouldn't be able to fly. What a disaster. Every pilot was needed to defend munitions factories, industry and airfields – not to mention the civilian population from the Luftwaffe. But there was nothing he could do. He expected a dressing down from his squadron leader for becoming unfit for service because of a fight and he'd probably be punished. His only consolation was that he'd be convalescing at Priory Hall.

His friend, Archie Cavendish, had suggested he stay with him in Hornchurch, but Luke knew Archie's sister, Vera, would be there and she was someone Luke could only take in small doses. She was confident, loud and ... well, frankly embarrassing, with her over-familiarity. Archie hadn't needed to tell him Vera had set her sights on him – she'd made it obvious – but he was just as determined she would never be more than an acquaintance. It was tempting to spend time in Hornchurch with Archie who was also unable to fly at the moment having been shot down several days before. He'd been remarkably lucky although his windscreen had shattered resulting in lacerations to his hands, and until they healed, he'd be grounded. Other than that, he'd escaped unscathed. However, Joanna had invited Luke to Priory Hall, and he'd jumped at the chance. He barely dared to admit to himself the real reason, telling Joanna it would be a good opportunity to spend some time with Lexie. But in unguarded moments, Samira, with her long, shiny, black hair and her intelligent, dark eyes filled his thoughts.

He had no right to play with Samira's emotions like Riccardo had played with Lexie's. As a pilot, he had very little to offer her except worry and possible heartache if he was shot down. It had been his intention to avoid a meaningful relationship until the war was over and so far, that had been easy because although he knew many girls, no one had interested him. In fact, he was beginning to wonder whether there was something wrong with him. He was totally in control of his emotions, unlike Archie who fell in love with a new girl each week. But it seemed it had been an illusion that he was master of his feelings because, from the first time he'd seen Samira, he hadn't wanted to take his eyes off her. Not surprising, as she was indeed beautiful. He'd assumed she'd be vacuous and vain, like most of the stunning girls he'd met but when he'd driven her to Essex, he'd discovered she was thoughtful, warm and, he admitted to himself, totally bewitching. As much as he'd have liked to have switched his feelings off, he stood as much chance of being able to do that as he was to see the lights above his head clearly.

For the next few days, he'd have the opportunity to spend time with her, even if he'd have to keep his distance. There'd be no more shared walks to watch the sunset and definitely no time spent alone together – he wasn't sure he'd be able to hide his feelings for long if she were to look at him the way she had when he'd been about to kiss her before. He closed his eyes and tried to imagine what it would have been like had Lexie not disturbed them.

When he opened his eyes, he could still see twice as many lights above his bed as he knew there were, but he consoled himself with the thought that as long as his vision was playing tricks on him, he would be able to stay at Priory Hall and at least be near Samira.

Ben picked Luke and Lexie up from the hospital once the doctors had discharged Luke and brought the dishevelled pair home in the car. Lexie had been at the hospital since Luke had been admitted the day before and had hardly slept, so her clothes were crumpled, and her hair was unusually unkempt. Luke's face was swollen, cut and bruised – so much so, that one eye was almost completely closed and when Lexie had helped him from the car, he limped to the front door. The welcoming committee greeted them warmly and Joanna had to warn Faye and Mark not to climb over Luke like they usually did, in case they hurt him. Joanna hugged Lexie drawing her into the hall and restrained the children while Luke entered. Samira stood back, keeping out of the way. She'd had to stop her hand flying to cover her mouth in shock when Luke had first got out of the car, and she longed to go to him. But what was the point of that? There was nothing she could do to help him heal faster, and the kisses she longed to place on his face would do nothing but cause him pain. And of course, she would merely be demonstrating her childishness and inexperience in front of everyone who would surely know a young, dashing and devastatingly handsome pilot would not have time for her.

"Isn't it wonderful Luke's back!" said Faye pulling at Samira's hand. "Come and say hello!"

"It's probably best to let him rest, darling. He'll be tired and in a bit of pain for a day or two," Samira said.

Neither Lexie nor Luke appeared for dinner much to Faye's disappointment.

"But I wanted to hear some stories about flying a plane," she said.

"Perhaps in a day or so, poppet," said Joanna. "Luke needs time to rest and heal. I can't imagine how he could have sustained such bad injuries from one blow. And the mess at the house was unbelievable. It looked like there'd been a dreadful fight."

"Well, apparently, Riccardo hit him with such force over the head with a stool, it sent him crashing into the dresser," said Ben. "You know, we're going to have to be rather understanding with Lexie for a while. She blames herself because when she saw Luke, she screamed, and that was enough to distract him for a second. Riccardo took the opportunity and hit him. Lexie was stunned at the viciousness. I suppose Riccardo felt he'd been cornered. But really, that was no excuse."

"Well, at least they've caught him," said Joanna. "Constable Farmer said he got as far as Wickford. And they'll return Luke's motorbike tomorrow. Riccardo will be taken to a more secure prison camp, so we won't see him again. I was dreading the police having to question Lexie about her part in the escape of a POW but apparently, Riccardo told the constable he'd followed Lexie and she'd had nothing to do with him escaping. That's probably the only decent thing he's done since he's been here."

"Well, it's one less thing to worry about, I suppose. You know, it's lucky my mother's gone to stay with her sister for a while," said Ben. "She'd have a field day pulling Lexie to bits. I can hear her now calling her 'hussy' and 'harlot'!"

"What's a hussyanharlot?" Faye asked.

"Never you mind," said Joanna trying to suppress a smile. "Just don't say that ... er word, again."

Samira excused herself as soon as dinner was finished, saying she wanted to check on Lexie. It was true, and as she hadn't slept well the previous night, she also wanted to go to bed early. Quietly, she tiptoed into the bedroom.

"Don't worry, Sam," said Lexie, who was sitting up in bed. "You don't need to creep about, I'm not asleep. Every time I close my eyes, I see Riccardo with that stool raised above his head a split second before he hit Luke. If only I hadn't screamed, Luke wouldn't have looked towards me, and he might have dodged the blow. There was such anger in Riccardo's eyes. I've never seen him like that before. And that was probably my fault too because I was trying to make him take me with him."

"Take you with him? Where did you think you'd be able to go?'

"South America?" She didn't sound very certain.

"But how would you both have got to South America?"

"I don't know but we'd have worked it out. Two people can't be so much in love and have to live apart."

"But Riccardo wanted to go to Italy. You couldn't have gone there."

"I know, that's why I thought it best if we went to South America, then one day when this dreadful war's over, we could have gone back to Italy. But he just kept saying he needed to get home and one day he'd come back for me. I couldn't bear the thought of being without him."

Samira sighed.

"Lexie, there's something you need to know about Riccardo—"

"Have they caught him? Is that it?"

"Well, yes, but that wasn't what I need to tell you. I'm so sorry, Lexie, but the reason he was desperate to get back to Italy was to be with his wife and child ... I'm so sorry ..." She slid her arm around Lexie's heaving shoulders and held her tightly as she sobbed.

"He promised me we'd be together one day if I helped him get away from the camp and got him to the coast. How could I have been so foolish?" Lexie said finally when the tears had stopped.

"You weren't to know, Lexie. Love makes fools of everyone from time to time."

"And after all that, my heart's broken and Luke's almost blind. Why am I so stupid and headstrong?"

"Lexie, darling, in time, your heart will mend. They always do. And Luke's far from blind. He's just got double vision. The doctors are satisfied he'll make a full recovery.

"But what if the doctors are wrong?"

"Well, we'll deal with that if it happens. But let's look on the bright side for a moment, while he's in a bedroom along the hall, he isn't in the cockpit of a Spitfire facing goodness knows what. He's safe. Now, why don't you try to sleep? You've had a terrible few days and you must be exhausted. Things'll look better in the morning."

"What would I do without you, Sam? You're so wise and good."

Samira gave her a final hug, undressed and climbed into bed.

*Wise?*

Hardly. She hadn't seen enough of the world, or of life, to be wise. And *good?*

She wasn't sure anyone in the RAF would commend her for being thankful one of their pilots was temporarily out of action, so he remained safe.

But with her whole heart and soul, she was glad that for a few days at least, Luke wasn't in danger.

Over the next few days, Luke's cuts healed, and the bruises faded although his vision was still slightly impaired. He played with Faye and Mark and helped with light chores but other than at mealtimes when the family ate together, if Samira entered the room, soon after, he'd make his excuses and leave. If broken-hearted Lexie had noticed, she didn't say anything, and it appeared to be only Joanna who'd detected the tension. She'd taken Luke and Samira aside separately and tried to find out what had led to the strained atmosphere, but both denied there was a problem. Joanna wasn't convinced, but in the absence of any evidence, and given the denials of them both, she began to wonder whether her intuition was at fault.

However, Joanna's attention was diverted from Luke and Samira one morning to Lexie, who'd insisted on cleaning up the mess and paying for all the broken furniture and china, saying it was the least she could do to make amends for her earlier stupidity. Although Joanna told her it wasn't necessary, she thought it might help Lexie get over the whole incident. Samira had offered to help but Lexie had insisted it was something she had to do on her own and that the Land Girls needed Samira to drive the tractor and help with the harvesting.

Joanna cycled to the house to check on Lexie's progress, as she had insisted on cleaning the mess caused by her stupidity, and was disturbed to find her sitting on the floor sobbing quietly.

"Lexie, darling, what's wrong?"

It took a while before Lexie could speak.

"Oh, Joanna, I've made such a mess of things. Everything I touch falls to pieces. And I miss Riccardo. Or at least I miss what I thought I had with him. And I've hurt Luke and let you and Ben down and Joanna insists I needn't pay for the damage to her furniture; I don't deserve—"

"Shh! You mustn't think like that. You made a mistake, that's all. Come on, let's finish this together and then we'll think of a way of cheering you up."

"I don't deserve you being nice to me."

"Hush now and put your energy into tidying up. Ben's cousins are coming on Saturday, so this needs to be ready by then."

When they'd finished, Joanna made them each a cup of tea and suggested they go into the garden and sit in the shade of the apple tree. It reminded her of all the evenings she'd shared with Ben and the Plotlands neighbours years ago when they'd gathered in someone's garden during the long, summer evenings. Mr Franks had often played his accordion and there'd been singing and dancing, and food cooked over the fire. It would be wonderful to do something similar to take their minds off the war and to cheer up Lexie.

She decided to arrange a family picnic where they could all enjoy each other's company. Sunday, she decided, would be the day.

Joanna took Luke aside that evening and told him how she'd found Lexie in tears earlier.

"But I've told her I don't blame her."

"I know Luke, but she's so unhappy. Perhaps if you had another word with her?"

"Of course. I'll try."

"I'm going to organise a family picnic for Sunday. Perhaps that'll take her mind off things."

"That's a wonderful idea, Lexie loves a party. Should I ask Archie? He's splendid company and he's met Lexie a few times. They seemed to get on well enough."

"Do you think that's a good idea? She's only just getting over Riccardo."

"Oh, don't worry about Archie. He's got a girl for each night of the week, but he and I think along similar lines. We both know there's no point getting serious – not while the war's on."

"A girl for each night of the week? I'm not sure that's what Lexie needs right now."

"Don't worry. Archie won't lead her on. He always makes it clear he's a free spirit. Trust me, he'll cheer her up."

*Free spirit?* Joanna thought, how could either of these young men be so sure they could control their emotions? Several years ago, both she and Ben had tried to curb their feelings for each other – and both had failed. But if Luke thought his friend would amuse Lexie, then it might be worth it. And it would give Luke and Samira a chance to spend some time together. Perhaps they would sort out their differences. Whatever they were.

Samira got up early on Saturday morning. She wanted to walk into Laindon before breakfast to post a letter to her father, pick up a few groceries for Joanna and, if she had time, drop in to see the Land Girls. With her shoes in one hand and her handbag in the other, she crept along the upstairs corridor in her bare feet so that she didn't wake anyone. On the small landing halfway down the stairs, she stopped and opened her bag. She was so engrossed with checking she had her purse and ration book; she didn't see Luke walking upstairs. She looked up to see who was approaching and when she saw it was Luke, she stepped aside to give way to him. As she moved sideways, her foot slipped and she stumbled forward dropping her handbag which bounced down the stairs, spilling its contents. Before she followed the bag, Luke reached out and grabbed her with one arm, steadying her.

They looked at each other in horror at what might have been.

"Th ... thank you," said Samira.

"Are you all right?"

"Yes, I think so." She peered down the stairs at the bag in the hall below.

"That was close." He gently pushed her away from the edge of the stairs. "You're shaking. Are you sure you're all right?"

"I ... I'm a bit shocked, that's all."

"You're all right now," he said, wrapping his arms around her.

She closed her eyes. How safe she felt in his arms, even if she was only inches away from where she'd nearly fallen.

With Luke standing on the step below her, their eyes were on the same level, and he placed his cheek against hers. Samira could feel his breath on her neck, and she suddenly realised that several buttons had popped open, and her blouse had slipped when he'd grabbed her, revealing one shoulder. Luke's fingers brushed her skin, slowly tracing a line from her ear, down her neck and across the top of her arm to the edge of her blouse. She shivered with delight as he planted tiny kisses along the invisible line drawn by his finger. Tipping her head back, she closed her eyes and gave herself up to the waves of pleasure that rippled down her body, radiating from where his lips caressed the skin which would normally be covered by her blouse. She hadn't realised she was holding her breath, until the back door slammed, shocking them both.

He quickly drew the fabric back in place and fastened the top buttons, then kissed the indentation at the base of her throat.

"It's probably best not to be found like this on the stairs," he said smiling at her. "Can we talk later? I promised Ben I'd go to Romford with him this morning but as soon as I'm back, can we talk? Please?"

She nodded, unable to speak, unable to catch her breath.

Hurrying downstairs on quivering legs, she retrieved the contents of her handbag. With a quick look about to ensure they hadn't been seen, she hurried out of the door, the tang of his scent still filling her nostrils and the site of each kiss tingling with the memory.

Luke had been polite and remote since he'd arrived at Priory Hall, so what had changed? She'd assumed he'd been angry with her for not keeping an eye on Lexie. And pride had not allowed her to seek him out to ask – and if she was right, to apologise.

*Does it matter?* A tiny voice in her head whispered, perhaps this war will go on forever and sanity will never be restored. Will you look back and wish you'd grabbed each second of happiness while you could?

She placed her outstretched hand over her chest as if to hold Luke's kisses on her skin. Nothing had ever made her feel as alive or as valued before, and her senses were still spinning with delicious shock. Gran's warning about ultimately being alone had been meant to warn her against trusting anyone but if she never gave anyone a chance, she'd be sure to end up alone. Perhaps caution and common sense had no place in this war-torn world. Perhaps it was time to live for the moment.

Samira was so desperate to see Luke, she rushed back from Laindon without visiting the Land Girls' cottage. While she waited for him to return, she played with Mark and Faye, keeping them out of the kitchen so Joanna could prepare for the picnic without interruption.

"Will you wear your hair up tomorrow, like you do when you're working on the farm, Samira?" Faye asked. "I think it looks better down."

"Well, I hadn't given it much thought really, darling."

"Oh, but you must! It's going to be so exciting."

Samira ran her fingers through the young girl's chestnut curls. "And how are you going to wear yours?"

"Oh, tied back. Although it never seems to stay in place for long."

"Perhaps that's because you're always running about."

"I s'pose so."

"Why not just leave it like it is?"

"Luke's friend, Ernie's coming and I want to look nice. And Daddy's cousins are coming too."

"Ernie? Do you mean Archie?"

"Oh yes, that's right. I heard Luke ask Mummy yesterday if it was all right to invite him to the picnic. He said it would cheer Lexie up ... I still don't understand why she's so upset. And who's Riccardo?"

"Just one of Lexie's friends who had to go away."

"Oh, I see. Well, it'll be nice if the picnic does make Lexie happy. Luke said Archie's very good company and apparently, he won't lead her on because he's a free spirit. What's a free spirit, Samira?"

"I'm not sure, darling. It probably depends on what people are talking about."

"Well, all I know is that Luke says he thinks the same sort of things as Archie. He said they have girls every night of the week and neither of them is going to get serious about it – well, not while the war's on anyway. So, Luke must be a free spirit too."

"Are you sure he said that?"

"What? The free spirit part?

"No, the part about girls every night of the week?"

"Oh yes. I don't know what he meant, though. I thought they flew every night of the week. D'you think it's another one of the funny things they say in the RAF, like *Tally-Ho* when they see an enemy plane and *Pancake* when they mean they're going to land?"

"Possibly."

"Are you all right, Samira? Your voice sounds all funny."

Samira nodded and smiled. It was best Faye didn't hear her voice break and most importantly that she didn't see the tears that were threatening to spill down her cheeks.

So, there it was. Evidence that Luke was taking every opportunity to find happiness. If she couldn't be his special girl, was she prepared to be one amongst many?

# Chapter Fourteen

♥

"Where d'you want me to set up?" Ben asked. "Under the cherry tree?"

"We're not having a picnic in the garden," said Joanna fastening the lid of the picnic hamper. "We're going to get away from normal life – just for a few hours. We're going somewhere with beautiful views and peaceful woods ..."

"We are? Where did you have in mind?"

"One Tree Hill."

"Ah!" Ben was silent for a few minutes, then catching hold of Joanna's hand, he pulled her close to him and held her tightly. "We haven't been there for some time," he whispered.

"I know. This war is getting in the way of everything. But it's the perfect place for Lexie to relax and I've been worried about Luke and Samira. I think they've had an argument or something. I can't work them out. When one comes into a room, the other one leaves. And yet, there's no animosity that I can detect – quite the opposite, in fact. There are long, lingering glances when each thinks the other isn't looking. So, if they're thrown together, it might give them a chance to iron out whatever differences – or otherwise – they have. Luke only has double vision when he's tired, the rest of the time his sight is pretty much back to normal. When he sees the doctor next week, he'll be sent straight back to Hornchurch ... and ... well, who knows if we'll ever see him again? So, this may be the last chance for them to patch up whatever needs patching up. And it might make Samira feel more at home too."

"Don't you think she feels at home here?"

"Well ... yes ... it's just that she doesn't seem to have anywhere she can call home. I know she has family in India, but she rarely talks about where she once lived, and when I ask her, she says it was so long ago since she was there, she doesn't remember much. She certainly doesn't talk about it as if she misses it. The only other place she's been for any length of time is the convent and she never mentions that at all."

"Well, Jo, if anyone can make Samira feel at home here, it's you." He kissed the tip of her nose. "Right, I'd better go and get the car."

Ben parked at the bottom of One Tree Hill, and everyone climbed out and helped Joanna carry the picnic things further up the slope next to the edge of the woods. Mark and Faye ran off to play with Ben's cousin, John; his wife, Caroline; and three children who'd set up a noisy game of cricket at the bottom of the hill where the ground was level.

"Is your friend coming, Luke?" Joanna asked.

"He said he'd come if the bandages are removed from his hands, but he's always late, so I wouldn't expect him yet."

"Is that him?" asked Lexie pointing down the hill at a rapidly approaching car.

"Well, if it is, that'll be the first time I've ever known him to be on time for anything."

Archie pulled up next to Ben's car and leapt out to greet Luke at the same time as the passenger door opened and Vera got out, straightened her hat, and smoothed the skirt of her suit with gloved hands.

"Luke, darling!" she said, throwing her arms wide and teetering across the grass on her high-heeled shoes. "I couldn't wait to see you again. It's been so long, you naughty boy!"

"Who's she?" Joanna whispered.

"That's Archie's sister, Vera," said Samira.

"How d'you know?" asked Lexie.

"I saw her when Luke brought me here the first time. We stopped off in Hornchurch at Archie's house, and she was there."

"Luke's never mentioned her," said Lexie.

"But it looks like they know each other quite well," said Joanna.

"Yes, doesn't it? She can't keep her hands off him." Lexie began to laugh as Luke attempted to keep distance between them and Vera tried to press against him, resulting in them moving sideways.

"If she doesn't stop, they'll end up at the bottom of the hill in the middle of the cricket game. Hey, Luke," Lexie called, waving her hand. "I need help with this." She pointed at the picnic basket.

Luke unlinked his arm and after a brief word of apology, he ran to Lexie.

"Here, just move it to the other side of the rug. I didn't really want a hand, but it looked like *you* needed one. Why on earth did you invite her?" Lexie whispered.

There was no opportunity to reply because Archie was nearby and seconds later, despite her high heels, Vera joined them.

"Well, at least the children are enjoying themselves with John and Caroline," said Ben as he helped Joanna carry the empty picnic basket back to the car. "I know it's not what you planned."

"Not what I planned? It's a disaster!" said Joanna crossly.

"But Lexie seems happy."

"I understand Archie is a womaniser. Not only that, but he's a pilot too, and this may be the last time we ever see him. I just wanted to cheer

Lexie up. The last thing I wanted was for her to replace one catastrophe with another."

"But at least she seems happy."

"Well, yes, I'll grant you that. But poor Samira. She seems so sad and lost. And what about poor Luke having that woman grab him whenever she gets the opportunity?"

"Poor Luke? What about the rest of us having to put up with her loudness? Doesn't she ever shut up?"

"Oh, Ben!"

"Seriously, Jo, she's bruised my eardrums."

"Stop joking, darling. We need to do something."

"Well, I can think of a way for Luke and Samira to get a bit of peace and quiet, but it means you and I will have to suffer more trauma to our eardrums ..."

"I'm listening ..."

"Suggest they go for a walk."

"*That's it? That's your idea?* But Vera will just go with them."

"Not if you suggest they go into the woods and find the well ... That ghastly woman is far too vain to risk getting her shoes dirty."

"Ah!" said Joanna slowly. "Yes! Very clever, Mr Richardson. It's definitely worth a go."

Samira glanced at her watch.

How much longer would this dreadful afternoon last?

After they'd finished eating, Archie had taken Lexie for a drive in his car. John, Caroline, and the children were picking blackberries at the bottom of the field; their excited shouts drifting up the hill to Luke, Vera and Samira who were sitting on the rug. Joanna and Ben were tidying away the picnic things but seemed to be spending a lot of time packing them in the car boot, then rearranging them.

At least Samira wasn't expected to participate in the conversation. Vera's attention was totally on Luke, her body turned towards him, her face lighting up on the few occasions he commented on anything she said.

Samira watched the children at the bottom of the hill, working their way along the hedgerow, screaming excitedly when they found a bush heavily laden with fruit.

If only she'd gone with them and left Luke and Vera alone. It wasn't too late ...

Ben and Joanna returned, hand in hand, and to her dismay, Ben suggested they go for a walk and find a well which he and Joanna knew of in the woods.

"It's quite a difficult walk, though ..." Ben said looking at Vera's high-heeled shoes.

"So, if you want to stay here, Vera, I'd love you to give me some beauty tips," said Joanna. "It's so hard with all the shortages and rationing, but you seem to have found a way of looking lovely."

"Thank you. That's very kind but I'm sure I can manage in the woods. I'd be very happy to give you a few of my secrets when I get back though."

Vera teetered after Luke and Samira who'd already disappeared into the undergrowth.

"Luke, wait for me!" Vera called as she hurried after them.

"Don't worry about me, Luke, I can easily go for a walk on my own," Samira said.

"No! Please wait!" he placed a hand on her arm "I've been desperate to talk to you, Samira. Where have you been? Please don't leave me alone with that woman."

Suddenly Vera screamed and began to wail.

By the time Luke and Samira reached her, she was hobbling along holding her leg.

"What's the matter, what've you done? Have you twisted your ankle?" Luke asked.

"No!" she snapped. "I've torn my stocking on a thorn. Do you know how hard it was to get hold of this pair of silk stockings? And now I've ruined one of them."

"Well, Ben did say it was a difficult walk and you might not manage in those shoes," said Luke.

"I assure you I could climb a mountain in these heels. But no one mentioned thorns. And no one said anything about the wildlife." She swatted a wasp which buzzed around her head.

"It's probably attracted by your perfume," said Luke.

"Well, it can jolly well – Ow! It stung me!" She held her hand to her neck and looked at Luke in disbelief.

"It stung me!" she said again as if she simply couldn't believe an insect would dare summon the nerve to approach her, let alone pierce her with its sting.

"Right," said Luke, "I think we'd better get you back to Priory Hall and put some vinegar on that sting." For the first time since Vera had arrived, the life had come back into his voice.

Luke held the bramble branches back so Vera wouldn't tear her other stocking or clothes and helped her back to Ben and Joanna.

"You'll come with me, won't you, Luke?" Vera said when Ben offered to drive her home.

"No need," said Joanna quickly. "Look, your brother and Lexie are back. Let's ask him to take you to Priory Hall. Lexie can go with you; she knows where the vinegar is. Luke and Samira can help us clear the rest of our things away and get the children. Then we'll come back in our car."

"Yes, excellent idea," said Ben taking Vera's arm and leading her to Archie's car before she could object.

Archie was less than sympathetic. "Vinegar? That's an old wives' tale. Come on, old girl, I'll take you home. It's about time we were going."

Vera turned back to appeal to Luke, but he was already walking uphill to the picnic rug and didn't turn around until Archie hooted, and his car had turned the corner and disappeared.

Lexie waved until he was out of sight.

"Archie's charming," she said when she caught up with Luke. "And such a gentleman ... He's coming here to see me tomorrow too ..."

"Oh no!" said Luke. "I'm sorry but if he brings that woman back tomorrow, I'm going to be out – all day."

"Well, if she's that bad, why did you invite her?"

"I didn't. She invited herself."

"She didn't seem that bad."

"How would you know? You didn't have to listen to her. And if you take my advice, you'll be very careful with Archie. He's a great chap but he tends to spend a lot of time with the ladies – lots of different ladies. I'd hate to see you get hurt again, Lexie. If I'd known he wasn't going to behave, I'd never have invited him. Actually, I wish I hadn't, then that dreadful woman wouldn't have come."

"Stop being such a crosspatch, Luke! Archie is simply charming. A perfect gentleman. Come on, let's go and get the children. Joanna and Ben have packed up and are ready to go."

Samira helped Joanna and Ben fold the rug and put it in the car while Lexie and Luke went to fetch John, Caroline, and the children. When Luke returned, he was carrying Mark.

"I think he's overdone it; he's almost asleep," he said, putting the small boy in Ben's arms.

The following morning Luke was in the kitchen sipping tea when Samira entered. She paused, not sure whether it would be too obvious if she simply turned around and went back upstairs until he'd finished his breakfast.

Lexie was still asleep. Since she was going out with Archie, she'd decided to have a lazy day until she needed to get up and start preparing for her date. Samira had already heard Ben go out and Joanna was feeding the chickens.

"Samira, I was waiting for you. I wondered If ..." he paused, the colour rising slightly in his cheeks.

"Yes?"

"Well, I wondered if you'd like to come with me to find the well we were going to look for yesterday. Ben said it was okay if you took the day off ..."

"No, thank you. I don't think so."

"Please Samira. If you're angry I didn't talk to you on Saturday after we ... well, after you nearly fell down the stairs, Ben and I got held up and by the time we came home, Joanna said you'd gone to bed."

"I had a headache."

"But I was desperate to talk to you. And as for yesterday ... I tried to get you on your own. I can't believe Archie brought his sister, and I'm definitely going to have words with him for flirting so outrageously with Lexie."

"I thought that was how you pilots behaved. A girl for each night of the week ..."

"Well," he said slowly, "it's true that's what some pilots do, but not all of us. Archie and I agree on one thing – it's not fair to get attached to anyone special while we're at war. But as for having a different girl each night? That's not for me."

"It's not?"

"No. It's not," he said firmly. "So ..."

"Yes?"

"I'm going to try to find the well. Please would you come with me?"

"Well ... yes ... all right."

His face lit up.

"I'll see you outside in ten minutes," he said and rushed out.

*Don't read too much into it*, she told herself, he's simply curious about the well and doesn't want to go on his own.

Why someone should be so interested in a well she had no idea. But who cared? He'd asked her to go with him and she intended to enjoy it.

There was no time to change out of her work overalls, she could hear the motorbike engine revving on the drive; it seemed Luke was ready to go. He helped her climb on to the bike behind him and when he was satisfied she was ready, he roared down the drive and out on to the road.

She remembered the last time they'd driven down these lanes on their way to Plotlands when she'd feared finding Lexie with Riccardo. There had been dread mixed with the excitement of the ride but now, exhilaration at the speed of the bike and the closeness of Luke made her breath catch in her throat.

They dismounted and left the bike near where the cars had been parked the previous day and Luke led her to the gap in the undergrowth where Vera had been stung.

"Do you know where the well is?" Samira asked.

"Not a clue," he said, laughing. "So, we may be here for some time." He slipped his hand into hers, their fingers interlacing, and he smiled at her.

The moment was so perfect, she hardly dared breathe.

The slanting rays of the morning sun filtered through the foliage, casting spears of green light on the ground. This was surely an enchanted forest. And he was hers. Only as long as they remained in this emerald world, of course. Sooner or later, they'd find the well, or they would abandon the search, but just for now – he was hers.

"It's so peaceful here, it's hard to believe there's a war on," said Luke.

"When do you have to go back to Horn ..." she trailed off, angry with herself for forgetting Lexie had told her he didn't like discussing leave because he thought it unlucky.

He stopped and pulled her to him, encircling her with his arms.

"Too soon," he said sadly. "My vision's back to normal now, so as soon as I see the doctor on Wednesday, I'll be recalled ... I know I've no right to ask you this, Samira, but I wondered if ... it's just I can't stop thinking about you and I wondered if ..."

He leant forward and placed his forehead against hers.

"I know it's a lot to ask ... I can't promise you anything ... but I wondered if you'd wait for me?" he whispered.

"Yes. Oh, yes."

A thrill ran through her as he lifted his forehead from hers and, taking her face between his hands, he leant towards her, his lips touching hers.

Nothing in her wildest dreams had prepared her for the rush of passion that coursed through her body. How right it was that the first person to kiss her should be Luke, and that they should be miles from anyone in the middle of an enchanted wood.

"Here, you're cold," he said, taking off his leather jacket and placing it tenderly around her shoulders.

She held the lapels and breathed in the spicy, leather smell, not wanting to tell him that she had shivered from pure bliss – and not from cold.

"The rest of the world seems so far away, we could be the last two people on earth," said Luke, raising her hand to his lips. "And just for the record, there's nobody I'd rather be with." He paused. "I promised myself I wouldn't do this – I told myself I'd wait until the end of the war before I looked for someone special. But the truth is, Samira, I wasn't looking for anyone – I just found you. I hardly slept last night thinking about today, wondering if I dared let you know how I feel. I'll be back at the airfield in a day or so. I may not live to see next week but I longed to feel you in my arms."

"And I longed to be there, Luke. This war's turned everything upside down. I think it's better to spend a few days together – if that's all we're allowed – than never to have shared anything at all. All we can do is live for the moment."

He held her to him, and she laid her cheek against his shoulder, feeling the beat of his heart. They stood together, holding each other, aware of the impermanence of their world. Luke looked up and stared into the distance. Suddenly, he gasped.

"Look! It's there. We've found it."

She turned and followed his gaze through a gap in the trees into a small clearing.

"Are you sure? I was expecting something like a wishing well with a small roof and a bucket, not something so big."

Luke took her hand and led her towards the structure which sat in the middle of the clearing. Surrounding the well, was a circular building with a roof supported by smooth, round pillars and on top of the roof sat a dome, like an ancient temple.

"No wonder Joanna suggested we find it," said Samira. "Who on earth would believe they'd find something like that in the middle of the woods. Do you know what it's doing here?"

"Joanna said the water's full of minerals and a few years ago someone was selling it in bottles. He turned it into a sort of visitors' attraction, but he had to close it because there was some sort of contamination. Now it's abandoned. But she and Ben used to come here for walks. I think it was their special place."

"D'you think she's lent it to us?"

"I rather think she has," said Luke, pulling Samira close again and kissing her.

"This is the memory I'll take with me the next time my plane's wheels leave the runway ... until they touch down again. Our temple – our magic wood – and losing myself in your beautiful, exotic eyes."

# *Chapter Fifteen*

J oanna put a mug of tea on the table in front of Samira and placing
her hand on the girl's shoulder, she sighed.

What was there to say?

Samira looked up and smiled but her eyes were brimming; their
rims red and swollen with the tears she'd already shed. She strained
to hear Luke's motorbike, but she knew it had gone. He'd left five
minutes before, and she'd waved until he'd been out of sight. For
several minutes, she still fancied she heard the roar of his engine as he
passed through the quiet country lanes on his way to Hornchurch.
Now, in the kitchen, all she could hear was the ticking of the clock.

"Why don't you go and lie down, Samira, you look exhausted."
Joanna's voice was shaky, and Samira knew she understood the pain
of separation from a loved one.

With a sigh, Samira nodded and sipped the tea. Not because she
wanted it, but because Joanna had been kind enough to make it for
her. It was tasteless, and she wondered if anything would taste, smell
or have meaning again until Luke was back.

But Joanna was right; she knew she ought to catch up on some
sleep. She'd been awake almost constantly for two days. After Luke
had asked her to wait for him, they'd spent most of the day in the

woods. They'd sat on the low wall that separated the well from the surrounding portico, and they'd talked and kissed until they realised with surprise, the shadows were almost equal and opposite to where they'd been when they'd first arrived.

After dinner, they'd walked to the spot where they'd once shared a sunset, ignoring Joanna's delighted wink at Ben when she'd caught sight of them hand in hand. They'd talked more as the sun sank below the horizon, and for some time after, until it was almost too dark to see.

Lexie had been distracted by her date with Archie and hadn't noticed Luke and Samira's new closeness, nor how little time Samira spent in bed that night.

How could Samira sleep knowing she and Luke had one more day together and then they'd possibly never see each other again? She'd stayed with him in the drawing room until the early hours before returning to her bedroom, and then risen before Lexie, meeting Luke on the landing for an early morning kiss. After creeping down the stairs, they grabbed several apples and headed out of the house. Samira had clung on to Luke as he'd driven his motorbike down to the mouth of the River Thames, at Southend-on-Sea. There, they'd strolled along the promenade watching the tide recede to leave boats stranded on the smooth, shiny mud.

Later that night after the moonlit water had surged back across the mud to reclaim the boats, Luke had driven back to Priory Hall. He switched the engine off at the gates and wheeled the motorbike up the drive – the only sound, the crunch of the gravel and their low voices.

It was well past midnight and during the early hours, they'd sat on the enormous leather sofa in the drawing room, holding each other tightly – sometimes dozing, sometimes kissing. At five o'clock, Luke washed, put on his uniform, kissed Samira one last time and left.

When Samira finally went to bed, she didn't think she'd be able to sleep, so was surprised to wake up and find the afternoon sun shining on her face. She was tempted to turn over, close her swollen eyes again and seek oblivion but she'd have to get up sometime – she wouldn't be able to stay there until Luke came back.

Until he came back.

She wouldn't allow the words 'if he came back,' to enter her mind.

Once, she'd wondered if she was incapable of loving – if something was missing from her personality. Now she knew there'd been nothing wrong with her at all, she simply hadn't met the right man. But it was scant compensation knowing the proof she was normal, was that she'd fallen in love with a man whose life expectancy was measured in weeks.

Stop wallowing in self-pity. She squeezed her hands into fists and clenched her jaw. Would it have been better never to have met Luke?

I'd rather have loved him for just one day than to have never met him at all.

Then get up and carry on.

The telephone bell cut through the chatter of the Crew Room in RAF Hornchurch. Immediately, cards, chess pieces and books were dropped. As the orders to scramble were given, pilots sprinted to their Spitfires, parachutes were strapped on, engines were started, and the aeroplanes taxied for take-off. In minutes, the pilots of 'A' Flight were airborne on their way to patrol the coast near Dover, in an area dubbed 'Hellfire Corner'.

Luke felt ill. He'd hardly eaten any of the generous breakfast that had been served to all the pilots who were on 'readiness'. For some reason, swallowing had been difficult and despite the cold weather, he was sweating.

I'll be glad of the warmth when I hit the freezing temperatures at twenty thousand feet, he thought. He wondered if he was going down with 'flu. Perhaps he should have reported sick, but it was too late now; the earth was falling away below. He couldn't let the lads down and after all, he'd been feeling off-colour for a few weeks now. Not sick exactly, just very downhearted. And who could blame him? Despite the bluster and boasting of the other lads, there was a deep, underlying gloom. There'd been too many losses, too many good men had not come back. And then an audacious German aerial attack last month had resulted in many of the ground crew being shot and killed as well. To say morale was low, was an understatement.

Luke checked his instruments.

Would this war ever be over?

The last time he'd seen Samira, Ben's neighbour had visited. Mike Harold had a heart murmur, so had been unable to join up, and he'd spent the war farming acres of land adjacent to Priory Hall. He was an agreeable man – funny and engaging and he obviously thought a lot of Samira. Luke had watched his eyes follow her when she was in the room. Not that Samira noticed, but still ... She deserved someone who could give her stability and love.

What could Luke give her? Love – that was certain, but for how long? Might today be the day he didn't return? Each time he took off, the odds against him meeting an accident in the air increased. He had no right still being alive ...

The cloud was dense and low, and Luke realised he'd lost sight of the other planes from 'A' flight. Suddenly, from above, a German Messerschmitt 109 dived at him firing in short bursts and Luke banked sharply to the left, turning skilfully so that within seconds, he had the enemy plane in his sights. He fired and seconds later, it exploded, disintegrating as it cartwheeled through the air in a blur of thick, black smoke and brilliant flames.

Before Luke could turn his plane back on course, another Messerschmitt climbed towards him from the rear, firing a hail of bullets. Flames erupted from the nose of Luke's aircraft like a crimson flower. Instantly, the cockpit filled with oily, choking smoke.

This is it. It's all over. Oh, Samira ...

Petrol. Dripping. Splashing over him.

Get out!

How many seconds before his clothes ignited?

Luke could see nothing. He dared not breathe. Instinct took over. He swung the aircraft onto its back.

One chance. He had one chance.

Take it! Take it!

Fumbling with his harness, he released himself and opened the hood.

A blast of icy wind tore at him.

Tumbling. Spinning. Falling through the sky. Groping for the ripcord.

Please! Please! Let the parachute deploy!

Freezing air rushing past, numbing all sensation. Its roar filled his ears as he plummeted towards the ground.

Luke closed his eyes. Impact was imminent. He didn't want to see ...

Blessed darkness.

Then a violent jerk as though a giant hand had seized his ropes and tugged him upwards. With a crack and a roar, the canopy filled with air, and Luke gripped the lanyards, hope renewed. But once again, he plunged, out of control, the wind whipping him, blowing him sideways. To his left, a fireball plunged towards earth – all that was left of his aeroplane.

Samira.

Blackness.

The first thing Lexie and Samira did on arriving home from working on the farm each evening was to check the hall table for the post. Samira breathed a sigh of relief when she saw the familiar blue envelopes addressed in Luke's handwriting, and silently gave thanks when Lexie received a letter which made her face light up with pleasure. If anything happened to Luke, it would be Lexie who would hear first – either from Archie or from her parents, and Samira would know instantly if something was wrong with Luke.

The war seemed never-ending with its shortages and endless struggle, and, in a few days, it would be the first anniversary of her and Luke finding the well at One Tree Hill – and each other. Since he'd gone back on active duty, they'd spent all the time they could together, although the snatched days didn't come often enough, nor last long enough.

Luke had visited the previous week, but he'd been worn out. Perhaps *burnt out* might be a better description. There was the usual sadness when he'd left but Samira felt something had changed.

Of course, he's changed, she told herself fiercely, he's facing the prospect of an agonising death most days. How could he not have changed from the carefree young trainee pilot to the flying ace he'd become?

But it hadn't affected Archie as deeply.

"Bravado," Lexie had said when Samira asked her why Archie appeared to be untouched by the war. "When you get to know him, he's kind and gentle and not like the overconfident, upper-class idiot he pretends to be."

Are they all pretending? Samira wondered. Was that how pilots kept going, day after day?

Samira longed to ask Luke, but she knew it would have to wait until she could speak to him face to face and she had no idea when that might be. She held out little hope they'd spend their first anniversary together.

First anniversary.

One whole year of being together, while actually spending most of the time apart.

Lexie was in a similar position. Against all odds, and despite their best intentions, Archie and Lexie had fallen in love. They too had seen little of each other. But after Lexie's previous liaison with Riccardo, she was reassured by Luke who reported that Archie's philandering ways were in the past. Samira was pleased at her friend's happiness, and she was also glad it meant Lexie could no longer object to Luke falling in love with her.

"There's one for you, Sam." Lexie tapped the blue envelope with the letter opener and then sliced open Archie's letter. Samira snatched up the letter, but before she could open it, the telephone rang and Lexie, who was closest to it, answered.

It was Archie.

"Hello, darling, I'm so glad you rang—" She stopped mid-sentence; her face turning white.

"No!" she whispered. "Please no! Where is he? Oh, no!"

She let the receiver fall and Samira could hear Archie's voice coming from the speaker.

Grabbing it, she held it to her ear. "Archie, are you there? It's Samira. What's happened?"

Had time slowed down? Or was she trying to fend off the words she'd dreaded for almost a year?

"I'm so sorry, Samira – Luke's been shot down. They've found his plane but ... but not Luke."

Samira spotted Archie's car swing through the gates of Priory Hall. He accelerated up the drive, the rear of the car fishtailing as he braked, flinging gravel in the air.

Samira sank on to her bed.

She couldn't bear to go downstairs to see him. It would be too painful. A reminder of what she'd lost. Burnt out pieces of Luke's plane had been found in a field in Kent – but there had been no sign of his body. At first, it was hoped he'd parachuted to safety but after five days, there had been no word.

And as each day passed, Samira's hope dwindled until now, none remained. She simply felt numb. Empty.

When Samira had first arrived at Priory Hall, she'd shown Joanna the four black, velvet bags that had been in Gran's hatbox. She'd wondered if she'd done the right thing when she saw tears course down Joanna's cheeks. After reverently picking them up, Joanna had turned them over and over, caressing them.

"My mother made these. I always knew Aunt Ivy had taken them." Joanna shook her head in disbelief. "She was a hard woman. I'm so glad she didn't treat you like she treated everyone else, Samira."

"I've no idea why, but she seemed to trust me. She told me several times that people come into your life, but they always let you down and, eventually, everyone ends up alone. Do you believe that?"

"No, Samira, I don't believe that. I think she was a sad woman who pushed everyone away, so she was lucky to have you there at the end. Not everyone ends up alone. Really, they don't."

But Gran's words now echoed through Samira's mind "People will come into your life and people will leave, but trust me, they'll let you down and, in the end, you'll be alone."

Luke hadn't let her down. He would have stayed with her if it had been possible. But in the end, the result was the same – she was alone.

Pulling the pillow over her head to keep out the delighted shrieks that accompanied Archie's arrival, Samira was surprised when the door burst open, and Lexie ran in.

"He's alive!" she shouted. "Sam! Get up! Luke's alive. Archie says he was found a few days ago. There was an administrative mix-up but now they know where he is. He's in hospital."

Lexie phoned the hospital in Folkestone and spoke to the ward sister while everyone stood around her straining to hear the news.

"Complications? What sort of complications?" Lexie asked and frowned as she listened to the reply. "So, when can we visit him? ... I see ... Well, is it all right if I phone back tomorrow for more news? ... I see ... Thank you."

She replaced the receiver on the cradle and looked at the expectant faces.

"Well, apparently, he injured himself badly when he landed, and he's broken his arm. He was also hit by shrapnel, but the sister said everything will mend."

"You mentioned complications." Samira held her breath.

"Sister wasn't sure. She said they're doing tests now but some of the swelling isn't going down and they don't know why."

"It's probably just the docs being overcautious," said Archie putting his arm around Samira's shoulders. "Don't worry. Luke's tough. And as soon as they know what's wrong, we'll all be down to Folkestone like a shot. That's why I came. I thought we could all drive down to see him, but it appears we can't today. Anyway, I've got three days' leave, so perhaps we can go tomorrow – assuming it's okay."

But the next day, when Lexie telephoned Sister Marlowe, she was told Luke wasn't strong enough to have visitors, and that they were still carrying out tests. Samira's earlier elation started to turn to despair. Something was very wrong.

In the end, you'll be alone.

The words cast a shadow over her heart.

Lexie had gone to bed several hours earlier with a headache although now, she was having nightmares. She muttered and mumbled, turning from side to side. Of course, it was hardly surprising the recent events had broken through into her dreams.

Had Samira been able to sleep, she too might have experienced nightmares, but she'd been awake for hours, her hands crossed beneath her head, staring up at the ceiling. Despite the chill in the air, Lexie pushed back the bedcovers and Samira tiptoed over to her. Would it be better to leave her to her nightmares or to waken her? Lexie's teeth were chattering so Samira pulled the bedclothes over her and smoothed her forehead, trying to calm her without waking her up but when she felt the cold film of sweat, she knew something was wrong.

Lexie opened her eyes. "Sam," she croaked. "I feel dreadful. My head feels like it's going to explode. I don't feel right at all."

"Shall I wake Joanna?"

Lexie nodded. She shivered violently.

Joanna arrived with a thermometer and cupping her hands around Lexie's face, gently pressed her neck. Lexie groaned.

"I think it's mumps," said Joanna. "It's like what Mark and Faye had a few weeks ago although they didn't have it as badly as this. I assumed everyone in the house had caught mumps when they were young. You've had it, haven't you, Samira?"

"Yes, I caught it from my brother years ago."

"We'd best ask Archie later."

"And Luke," said Samira. "If Lexie hasn't had it, it's likely Luke hasn't either."

"You're right. The incubation time's about two weeks, so it's possible. That might explain his unusual swelling. I don't suppose mumps is the obvious diagnosis when a pilot has crashed. I'll ring the hospital to let them know."

# Chapter Sixteen

Something was wrong.

Luke couldn't work out what it was, but something was definitely wrong.

What was he doing here? He looked from one side of the hospital room to the other, taking in the sister and the doctor who were standing at the end of his bed.

He recalled the jerk of his parachute as it opened, and then he remembered tugging at the lanyards to try to steer it away from the farm buildings below while praying his blazing plane wouldn't cause any damage, and then, just as the realisation came that the wind was blowing him towards a barn, he'd blacked out.

And now there was light – bright, clinical light, and with relief, he noticed there was no double vision such as he'd had the last time he'd been in hospital. He moved slightly and pain shot through his shoulder and legs making him gasp. At least, he thought he'd gasped. He was sure the noise had left his lips, but it certainly hadn't reached his ears. And now the doctor's mouth was moving as if he was speaking to him but there was no sound.

Luke lay in a silent world of pain.

"The patient's progress, sister?"

"He seems slightly more alert this morning, doctor. Certainly, he's no longer delirious. The swelling is subsiding but not as fast as I would have expected. The fracture, contusions and grazing all seem to be healing with no sign of infection."

"It's fortunate his family told us about the mumps. At least now we know why his swelling's so bad. It's jolly bad luck all the same."

"Yes, doctor, I understand he came into contact with an infected child at the same time as his sister, but she's nearly over it now. In fact, she wants to visit. I told her not to come until she's completely better."

The doctor wrote in his book, and taking his stethoscope, he moved towards Luke.

"And how are we this morning, Pilot Officer Jackson?" the doctor asked. "I'm going to listen to your heart. Just relax. Sister's going to give you something for the pain, would you like that?"

Luke frowned. "Doctor, I can't hear you. I can't hear anything at all. What's wrong with me?"

"Don't get agitated," the doctor said with a reassuring smile. "It will be all right," he added slowly.

"Do you think the loss of hearing is a result of his fall?" Sister asked.

"Possibly although I'm afraid, there may be another explanation. Occasionally, deafness is a side-effect of mumps. It's likely to be temporary. But since he's suffering so badly, there's another complication we can't rule out. In very few cases, there's a reduction in fertility. But let's not worry the patient too much. One thing at a time. Let's see how his hearing goes and then do some tests later."

The doctor placed the chest piece of the stethoscope over Luke's heart and nodded reassuringly. He smiled and mouthed 'Good' to Luke.

"All normal," he said to the sister. "We'll just have to wait and see now."

As they turned to go, Luke called, "Sister, please don't let anyone visit. I don't want to see anyone."

She nodded and smiled, "I understand," she said exaggerating the movements of her mouth so he could lip read.

Samira stared at the blue envelope. The postmark showed it came from Folkestone, but the writing wasn't Luke's neat script.

"He's probably asked one of the nurses to write it for him," Lexie said. "He may not be able to write with all his injuries. I wish he'd let us visit ... Why don't you open it, Sam?"

It was the sensible thing to do. But she had a feeling this letter heralded a change – and one that was going to bring her unhappiness.

Lexie had phoned the hospital every morning for an update on Luke's progress and each morning she'd asked when it would be possible to visit him. The sister had repeatedly told her Luke was too ill, but yesterday a different nurse had taken the call and let slip that Luke was refusing to have visitors.

"He wouldn't want us standing around looking at him and feeling sorry for him," she told Samira, but despite her explanation, Lexie had been subdued. Samira had written each day, sometimes twice a day but this was the first reply she'd received.

She sliced the envelope with the letter opener and pulled out the single sheet of paper.

"Sam, what's the matter? What does it say? You've gone completely white!"

Samira handed the letter to Lexie.

"Oh, darling, he doesn't mean it. He loves you. It can't be over!"

"He's discharged himself and asked me not to contact him again. I'd say that pretty much means it's over."

"Stupid, stubborn man! If he left the hospital yesterday, he'll be in Devon by now. If only we had a telephone at home. I'll ring the Post Office and get someone to fetch Mummy. She'll talk some sense into him. Or I'll go home and do it myself. Yes, we'll both go ..."

Samira shook her head. "I must respect his wishes, Lexie. I can't make him want me – and neither can you."

"This is wrong! You both belong together. I'll make him see ... I'll—"

"Please don't, Lexie," said Samira. "It's over. I just have to find some way of accepting it and move ..."

Moving on, however, proved to be easier than Samira had thought it would be. Not because she didn't think of Luke constantly, nor because she loved him any less, but because several weeks later, she found herself literally moving on.

Finally, after so many long, dreadful years, the war ended. There had been talk about the conclusion of hostilities for some time, but Samira had decided that until peace was declared, she wouldn't believe it.

However, on the eighth of May 1945, the country celebrated VE Day with street parties and celebrations. Ben suggested everyone go to London to wait outside Buckingham Palace to cheer King George and the royal family. However, Samira had stayed home on her own in case Luke travelled from Devon to Essex to celebrate with Archie and the other pilots in his squadron – or indeed with Lexie. Samira knew he wouldn't, of course, but at least she could stay home on her own rather than risk spoiling everyone else's fun. The day she'd longed for had finally arrived, but without Luke, it was bittersweet. This was supposed to be *their* time. The start of life together unhindered by wartime obligations.

The other reason she didn't want to go was because Mike Harold, the next-door neighbour, had asked if he could accompany the party to London. He'd made it clear he was fond of Samira, and she suspected he'd asked to join them because he thought she was going. He was a nice man, but she simply wasn't interested. It was Luke, or no one.

Since VE Day, Mike had become more persistent, inventing excuses to visit Priory Hall and when he came, he brought her flowers and small gifts.

"Simply tell him you're not interested, Sam," Lexie said.

"I've tried. But he doesn't listen."

"Well, if you don't tell him, I will. He's getting on my nerves keep hanging around."

"Lexie! Please don't hurt his feelings!"

Mike had called a few hours earlier to ask if Samira would like to accompany him to Chelmsford for lunch, but Lexie had answered the door and told him Samira was out.

The doorbell rang.

"Oh, honestly! That man is unbelievable. I told him you were going to be out all day. I'm going to sort this out once and for all!" Lexie marched out of their bedroom.

"Lexie! Be kind!"

Samira listened at the door, but she was puzzled when she heard a man's voice in the hall and Lexie telling the visitor she'd fetch Samira.

"Who is it?" she asked when Lexie entered the bedroom.

"Come and find out."

"Lexie! You haven't invited Mike in, have you?"

"Of course not! Come on, your visitor's waiting for you in the drawing room."

Samira followed Lexie downstairs.

It took Samira a few seconds before she realised the visitor was her brother, Vikash.

Samira noticed with relief he no longer treated her with the disdain he'd displayed after their mother had died. She was pleased to see the sulky boy had become a very handsome, engaging man, dressed in an expensive western-style suit. The letters that had passed infrequently between them had been formal and stilted, so it was a surprise to find him so charming.

"What are you doing in England, Vik?"

"I'm on a business trip to London. I don't know if you're aware, but I work with Uncle Rahul now, he's bought a tea plantation, and I've been looking for new business for him now the war's over."

"Why aren't you helping Papa run our tea plantation?"

"Well, I do," he said. "But I help Uncle Rahul too. Anyway, Papa is the reason I've come. He's not well at the moment."

Samira gasped. "Why didn't he tell me? Is it serious?"

"No. When I saw him last, he was recovering, but he asked me to come and see you while I was in London and persuade you to return with me. He misses you, Samira. So, will you come?"

"Well, this is all so sudden. When are you leaving?"

"Tomorrow. I sail from Southampton in the morning. And we need to leave here as soon as possible."

"You sail *tomorrow*?"

"Yes, I know it's short notice ..."

Lexie looked horrified; her eyes wide with shock. "What about ...?"

Samira knew she was thinking about Luke. But what about him? He'd made it clear he wasn't coming back. Perhaps this was the change she needed. She didn't belong here now. Of course, she wasn't sure what was waiting for her in India either, but if Papa was asking for her, then she ought to go.

"I'll pack," she said.

Lexie followed her upstairs. "Samira, Stop! You can't just leave like that."

"There's nothing here for me now, Lexie."

"*I'm* here," Lexie said. "And Joanna, Ben and the children love you."

"But you all have your own lives. You have Archie. Joanna's family have each other and the farm. I'm not sure where I belong. And if Papa is asking for me …"

"Yes, of course … of course, darling … I was just being selfish. But you will write, won't you? And you will come back once you know your father's all right?"

"Of course, I'll write," Samira said, avoiding the other question. "Lexie, I wonder if you'd be able to do something for me?"

"Anything."

"Please would you send a telegram to Papa to let him know I'm on my way? If anything happens to him, I'd like him to know I was on my way home."

"Yes, of course. I'll go into town as soon as you leave."

Samira looked out of the rear window until the car turned out of Priory Hall's gates into the lane, and she could no longer see the waving figures at the front door. Faye and Mark had clung to her crying, and Joanna, Ben and Lexie had hugged her tightly in turn with tears in their eyes. She too, had wept but with Papa asking for her, she had no choice. And Joanna had made it clear she would always be welcome at Priory Hall.

"Don't worry," said Vikash patting her hand. "As soon as we set sail tomorrow, it'll take your mind off your friends. So, tell me what you've been up to. We've got a lot to catch up on."

Samira was glad of the distraction. She focused on Vikash's face and avoided looking beyond him through the car windows to the hedges and cottages they passed. Not that she needed to see the familiar landmarks to know exactly where they were – she knew every turn and junction, every dip and rise of the road. During her time in Priory Hall, she'd passed through those lanes on her bicycle with Lexie, on foot with the Land Girls, on the tractor with the POWs and of course ... on a motorbike with Luke. After a while, with both relief and sadness, she realised the roads were no longer recognisable and she knew she'd finally left Essex. As she watched the scenery speed past the car, she noticed that periodically, the turbaned-driver's eyes seemed to follow her in the rear-view mirror. She wondered if he was just keeping a watchful eye out for her and Vikash, like a loyal servant. There was no softness in his eyes, and they seemed to be exclusively focused on her.

*Don't be ridiculous*, she told herself. He's probably one of Father's servants whose duty was to make sure she got back to India safely.

But when they arrived in Southampton, Samira learned the servant, who was called Tariq, wasn't one of her father's servants – he worked for Uncle Rahul, and furthermore, her uncle was waiting for her and Vikash, and would accompany them to India on the *Aurora Crown*.

Uncle Rahul had been painstakingly polite when he met her and told her he'd had new clothes and jewellery delivered to her luxury cabin and that she was not to worry about anything because he, Tariq and Vikash were there to make her journey as comfortable as possible. He led them onto the ship where the chief steward met them and escorted them to their cabins. Samira's proved to be luxurious, indeed.

"We will be dining with the captain this evening, Samira, so please dress appropriately and be ready at seven sharp."

After a long soak in the bath, Samira dressed. The outfits Uncle Rahul had given her consisted of traditional Indian dress of *shalwar* –

baggy trousers which fitted tightly around the ankle, and *kameez* – a long shirt, and a silky scarf. They were colourful and expensive fabrics, but Samira preferred the clothes she was used to, and selected a smart navy-blue dress and matching shoes.

There was a knock at the door at exactly seven o'clock but when Samira answered it, she found Tariq and not Uncle Rahul as she'd expected. She squirmed with embarrassment as he looked her up and down, frowning.

"Come!" he said and led the way to the dining room where Vikash and Uncle Rahul, dressed in robes and turbans, were waiting for her.

Her uncle frowned. "Why are you not dressed appropriately as I instructed? Go and get changed!"

Samira's jaw dropped open. She hadn't been spoken to in such commanding tones since she'd been at school. Vikash took her arm and steered her out of the dining room.

"Uncle Rahul doesn't approve of women wearing western clothes, Samira."

"But it's up to me what I wear." Her stomach knotted at the thought of spending the entire voyage with her unreasonable uncle.

"Yes, yes, of course, it is, but he spent a lot of money on those clothes. And he probably wants to show his niece off to the captain. Would it be too much to ask you to wear them?"

"Well, I suppose not but I don't think I'm going to feel very comfortable. I'm not used to wearing anything like that." To be fair, it wasn't too much to ask and once she'd explained to her uncle, hopefully, he'd see her point of view.

Uncle Rahul smiled when she reappeared, and proudly introduced her to Captain Rigby, fussing over her until she was seated at the table – then promptly forgot her. She ate in silence while her uncle chatted to the captain, and Vikash talked to a couple from New York. When any of the guests tried to converse with her, Uncle Rahul took over the conversation and answered for her until she was finally ignored. After dessert, Uncle Rahul summoned Tariq with a click of his fingers and told him to escort Samira back to her cabin.

"Make sure my niece has everything she desires," he said loudly to Tariq, and the couple from New York looked at him with admiration.

Vikash topped up his wine glass and avoided her gaze. Had he noticed she'd spent the meal in silence? Perhaps that was what he considered normal. Well, at least, when she arrived home, Papa wouldn't treat her like that.

Samira told Tariq she wanted to stroll along the deck so she could see the shore before they set sail the following morning. He said nothing but his brows drew together. She knew he wasn't happy, and he followed her closely – almost like a bodyguard, she thought.

It would be a relief when she made some friends with whom she could spend time during the long voyage to Bombay and didn't have to rely on Vikash or Uncle. However, the chance of anyone talking to her with the forbidding figure of Tariq at her shoulder was slim. His turban lent him extra inches in height, and the baggy trousers, long shirt and cloak were reminiscent of a wicked vizier from *Tales of the Arabian Nights*. It wasn't beyond the realms of possibility that beneath his cloak, lay a sword or dagger. As soon as she was familiar with the ship, she'd insist he didn't accompany her anywhere. After all, she wasn't in danger, she didn't need a guard and she certainly wasn't used to having a servant. But she couldn't shake off the feeling that although Tariq seemed to have been assigned to serve her, he was actually watching her.

On arriving at her cabin, Tariq unlocked the door and let her in. She became aware she hadn't heard his footsteps leave, and a muffled cough told her he was still outside. What's more, he still had her cabin key. She opened the door to ask for it and found him standing in the corridor with his arms crossed.

"Please may I have my key?"

"No need," he said, staring stonily ahead.

She slammed the door and slid the bolt across. Tomorrow, she'd find her uncle and ask him to keep Tariq away from her. She'd lived through six years of war, and she could look out for herself.

There was a tap on the communicating door between her cabin and Vikash's.

"It's me," said Vikash. "I wanted to check you're well."

She opened the door.

"No, Vik, not really. I've been refused my own cabin key by a servant. And the last I heard, he was still outside my room."

"Yes. Uncle has ordered him to look after you."

"That's ridiculous! I'm perfectly capable of looking after myself."

"Well then, consider he's there to serve you."

"I don't need a servant. I'm used to fending for myself."

He raised his eyebrows in surprise. "Well, you'd better get used to it. Your life's going to be very different from what you're used to."

"Only while I'm in India ... and I don't know how long that'll be. From what I've seen of Uncle Rahul, it won't be long."

"He's fine once you get to know him. He just likes the traditional ways." Vikash looked down at the large ruby ring on his finger and twisted it round and round.

"Perhaps you're right," she conceded. "And I must admit I'm looking forward to spending time with Papa."

"You never know, you might decide to stay for good."

"I might." She had the feeling Vikash was steering the conversation.

He nibbled his lower lip. "Ah, well, I suppose I might as well tell you now. Uncle Rahul has suggested a husband for you—"

"He's *what?*" The knot in Samira's stomach tightened.

"Yes, now don't panic. I know that's not how it's done in England but before you make a decision one way or the other, let me show you his photo."

"Is that what this voyage is all about?" Samira shivered as an icy sensation trickled down her spine.

"Of course not!" Despite his indignant words, he blushed.

"Well, I can't believe you haven't mentioned something as important as this already."

"It's just a suggestion. You don't have to marry him. But he's very wealthy and you might decide it's a good option. Look ..." He took the photo from his wallet and held it out to her.

The prospective bridegroom was sitting in a studio with members of his family around him surrounded by potted palms. In front of him sat two young boys on cushions and a young girl stood next to his ornate chair, with her hand on his shoulder – presumably they were his brothers and sister. Seated next to him, was his father, a distinguished man with grey moustache and beard.

"Who is he?" she asked.

"Neelam Banerjee. He's one of Uncle Rahul's business associates."

Samira guessed he was about thirty years old and – if it was possible to tell from such a small photograph – he was one of the most handsome men she'd ever seen. Everything about him was perfect: the shape of his face, the intelligent-looking eyes – everything. Despite the traditional Indian dress, she could see Neelam was trim and well-proportioned. He was a man who'd turn women's heads.

"What d'you think?" Vikash twisted the ruby ring around his finger again.

"Well, he's very handsome, but ..."

"You'll consider it?"

This was too much. She would not be manoeuvred by her brother or her uncle. "No! I've no wish to marry. And certainly not someone chosen for me by my uncle."

"But you just said he's handsome." Vikash's face hinted at the sulkiness she knew from their youth.

"He is, but I want more from a husband than good looks."

"Why don't you meet him when we get home? You might find you like him. You might find you fall for him." Vikash's voice was wheedling.

"No, definitely not." What was the matter with her brother? Why was he so keen on pressing this ridiculous idea?

Vikash scowled. "Well, why don't you keep the photograph? You might change your mind."

In the morning, Samira rose early, took a bath and was about to dress when she noticed her suitcase was missing. She'd removed her toiletries and jewellery the previous evening and the only clothes she'd unpacked had been the navy-blue dress and shoes she'd put on before Uncle Rahul had told her to change. Neither the dress nor the shoes, however, were in the wardrobe where she'd put them. She had no choice but to wear shalwar and kameez to go to breakfast and then to go on deck and wave goodbye to England as they set sail.

When she told Vikash her luggage was missing, he turned away from her and stared fixedly at the shore.

"Vik, do you know what happened to my clothes?" she demanded.

"Well, Uncle Rahul doesn't approve of western dress, so I assume he got Tariq to remove them."

"How dare he!"

"Well, to be fair, Samira, he spent a fortune on silks, satins and jewellery for you, to replace your clothes."

"I don't care! They were mine! You're wearing a western suit. Why is it all right for you, but not for me?"

"Because ... well, because. I'm a man. That's all. Don't upset him, Samira. Trust me, you'll regret it." His voice was low and menacing.

Vikash was being melodramatic, she was sure. Uncle Rahul was a charismatic man, and her brother was obviously deeply in awe of him. When they arrived home, Papa would allow her to buy whatever clothes she wanted but, meanwhile, it was probably wise to do as Uncle wished. He had, after all, paid for her passage in a luxury cabin and for all the new clothes and jewellery. She ought to be courteous and grateful.

During the next few days, the seas were stormy and mountainous, and Samira kept to her cabin. She felt too ill to worry about Tariq's constant presence outside her door, or his supervision when the steward brought her light meals and cleaned her cabin. At least she hadn't seen Uncle Rahul. Vikash was also seasick, and she didn't see much of him either.

One morning she woke to find the winds had subsided and the sea was once again calm. She decided she would walk on the deck and get some fresh air. When she opened the cabin door, Tariq was waiting.

"I'm going for a walk – on my own." She walked quickly along the corridor. He increased his pace as he followed.

She stopped and turned. "I'm quite all right, thank you. There's no need to come with me."

Tariq appeared to look straight through her.

Samira continued to the deck. It was pleasant to be in the fresh air, but the oppressive presence of the servant unnerved her, and she decided to go back to her room and write to Lexie. She'd already written several letters and had asked the steward to post them when they'd docked at Santander. The letters should now be on their way to England.

The *Aurora Crown* would shortly arrive in Gibraltar, and she'd go ashore and post any letters herself. It would probably mean being trailed by Tariq, but at least she'd walk on solid ground again and it would be lovely to sightsee. Perhaps Vikash would come too.

She returned to her cabin. It was the only place she could be free of Tariq. It didn't matter how many people she smiled at and greeted, everyone seemed intimidated by the servant, and it was unlikely she'd make any friends on this voyage.

While she'd been on deck, John, her steward had gone into her cabin to clean, and was in the bathroom when she returned. Whenever Samira had been in her room and John had arrived to clean, Tariq always supervised, but this time, he was unaware the steward was already in the cabin.

"Morning, miss. And where's the big man?" John asked.

"Tariq? Oh, he's outside."

"Don't you mind him always being there, miss?"

"Yes, I do, but my uncle insists. As soon as I get home, I won't have anything more to do with him. Do you want me to go out again so you can clean?"

"No, don't worry, I've nearly finished."

Samira sat at the desk and got out the writing pad.

John hovered uncertainly in the doorway to the bathroom. "Begging your pardon, miss, but you do realise those letters you asked me to post didn't leave the ship?"

That was disappointing. Lexie and Joanna would start to worry if they didn't hear soon. "Oh dear. Please could you bring them to me, and I'll post them in Gibraltar when we dock."

"No, you don't understand, miss, after you gave me each letter, the big man took them off me. I don't have them anymore."

The breath caught in Samira's throat. Tariq had taken her letters? How dare he? No, there must be a good reason. Perhaps he didn't trust the steward. "Perhaps he posted them himself?"

"He might have. But I don't think he's disembarked so far this voyage." John's brow wrinkled. "Please don't tell anyone I told you, miss. Your uncle will get me in trouble, and I need this job. If your letters were important, I could arrange to have a telegram sent."

Samira's thoughts whirled. Why would Tariq have taken her letters? That didn't make sense. But then, why would the steward make up such a story? Who should she trust? Her instincts told her John was more reliable than the servant who treated her with such contempt.

Yes, she'd trust him. "That would be wonderful, thank you, I'll write a message. And don't worry, I won't say anything about my letters."

John finished making her bed and then tapped on the communicating door between Samira and Vikash's cabin.

"What's up?" It was Ted, the steward who was cleaning Vikash's cabin.

"Let me in, mate. The big bloke's back and I don't reckon he'll be happy about me being in here on my own with the lady."

John took the slip of paper from Samira and winked. "I'll let you know if you get a reply. If the big man's there, I'll leave a message tucked inside your fresh towels. And chin up. You'll soon be married and won't have to put up with the likes of him anymore."

"Married? No, I'm definitely not getting married. I'm going home to see my father."

John's eyebrows rose and he tipped his head to one side. "That's not what your uncle said, miss. I overheard him talking to Captain Rigby. He said you were engaged."

"Yeah, that's right," said Ted. "The captain told the chief steward you'd be getting married, and before you disembarked in Bombay, we'd have to arrange a party for you."

The two stewards went into Vikash's cabin and Samira quietly closed the communicating door. Her heart was thumping so loudly, the sound filled her ears. Where was Vikash?

She waited several hours for her brother to come back and had almost decided to go and look for him when she heard noises coming from his room. She'd thought carefully about how she was going to phrase her questions to protect John and Ted before she knocked on the shared door.

"If you don't mind, Vik, I'd like to talk to you about the proposed marriage."

"Of course!" His eyes opened wide in delight, and she wondered if he assumed she was about to tell him she'd agree to it.

"Did you tell Uncle I was considering the marriage?"

"Not exactly." His voice was hesitant.

"But you didn't tell him I'd refused."

"No, I thought you might like longer to consider it. Just think, you won't have to worry about anything ever again if you marry into the Banerjee family. Uncle wants this. It would be best if you agreed."

"That's the second time you've said something like that, Vik. Why would it be best? Best for whom?"

"All of us." He broke eye contact and twirled the ruby ring around his finger.

"Why does my marriage concern you?" Samira studied his face. She may not have seen him for many years, but she remembered how bad he'd been at bluffing when he was a young boy. He didn't appear to be any better now.

"I didn't want to have to worry you with this, Samira, but when Papa was unwell, Uncle took over the running of the plantation and now our family owes him."

"Owes him money?" She hadn't expected that. So, what else had Vikash been hiding?

"No, not money exactly, it's more a debt of gratitude."

"So, you mean Uncle Rahul expects me to marry a man of his choosing because he did what most other people would have done – he helped his sister's family when they were in need?"

"Well, it's not quite like that. He doesn't *expect* you to marry. But it would please him. Is that too much to ask? I mean, what plans do you have for the future anyway?"

Samira was silent. She didn't have any plans at all. No home and no one special. Of course, her friends were wonderful, but they all had lives of their own. And other than them, the only people she had were Papa, Vikash and Uncle Rahul. Perhaps it was time she stopped thinking about what might have been and started concentrating on her family.

"So, you'll think about the marriage?" Vikash asked hopefully as she went back into her room.

"I'll consider it."

# Chapter Seventeen

T hat night, Samira dreamed of Luke.

She clung to him while they sped through the country lanes of Laindon on his motorbike; her hair and a long, silky scarf streaming behind her. The smell of his leather jacket and the fresh green scent of the country filling her nostrils. When they arrived at One Tree Hill, he helped her off the bike and taking her hands, he drew her into the woods towards the well. The simple dome had acquired a point and now resembled a minaret, and this – like the pillars and walls – was covered in blue and gold mosaics that sparkled and flashed in the dappled sunlight. Luke swung her off her feet and carried her into the temple, her arms clasped tightly around his neck and her face against his shoulder. She could feel the heat of his hands on her back, through the gauzy fabric of her *kameez*. Under the portico, he gently let her feet down and pulled her to him and she realised he was no longer wearing his uniform and leather flying jacket – he too was wearing *shalwar* and *kameez* and as their bodies pressed against each other, it was as though there was no fabric between them at all. He bent and kissed her neck and as the waves of pleasure rippled through her body, he began to undo the buttons of her *kameez* and slide it off her shoulders.

Luke's fair hair darkened until it was the deepest black, and when he looked up at her, she gasped as she realised she was staring into the dark and mysterious eyes of Neelam Banerjee.

Samira sat up in bed. The shock of her dream had wakened her, and she pulled the neck of her nightdress up, remembering how Neelam had peeled her *kameez* down over her shoulders. But while her cheeks burned with shame, the glow of desire still filled her body.

The rest of the night passed fitfully. She was afraid of sleeping again for fear of where her dreams would lead her – and with whom. By early morning, she'd made up her mind she would meet with Neelam. Where was the harm in that? And if she didn't like him, she simply wouldn't marry him.

Samira got ready quickly. It was early and Tariq had not yet taken up position outside her room. She slipped into the corridor and with her sandals in her hand, ran silently over the luxurious carpet. Thankfully, the decks were deserted, and the sunrise belonged to her. Far off, she could hear members of the crew talking and the chink of cutlery and china as the dining room was prepared for breakfast, but none of them had the time to lean against the rails and drink in the beauty of the dawn, as she did.

When she heard footsteps approaching, she assumed it was Tariq. She stared at the horizon, refusing to acknowledge him.

"Good morning, Miss Stewart, I trust you're enjoying the voyage. We haven't seen much of you at dinner. I hope you didn't suffer too badly during the storms?"

She swung around to find the captain smiling at her.

"Oh, good morning, Captain. I'm so sorry, I was miles away."

"Longing to be with your fiancé, I imagine."

"Well ..." She hesitated, not knowing whether to admit she wasn't sure about marrying or not.

"It's understandable to be nervous, Miss Stewart. Marriage is a big step. I'm very grateful to your uncle for inviting me to the wedding, by the way, it's a great honour."

Uncle Rahul had already started inviting guests to her wedding?

She smiled and hoped he assumed she was aware he'd been asked.

"And ..." he added, his eyes sparkling. "Your uncle told me to keep this quiet but I'm sure you'll be relieved to know your honeymoon has been settled."

"It has?"

"Yes, it will be our great pleasure to have you and your husband as our guests when we leave Bombay for Australia. We sail a few days after your ceremony, so it'll give you a chance to get to know your new family and then you'll occupy the bridal suite with no expense spared."

"Oh, I don't know what to say." She struggled to keep the smile on her face. Truly, she didn't know what to say. So much had been arranged and she hadn't made up her mind she even wanted to marry. It was suffocating. Suppose she decided against marrying Neelam? How could she possibly disentangle herself from arrangements that had already been made? She needed to plant doubts in people's minds.

"That's very generous of you, Captain but since I don't really know my husband-to-be, I wonder if his business might prevent him taking a honeymoon. I know he owns several tea plantations ..."

Captain Rigby looked puzzled. "I'm sure it'll be fine. Your uncle said he's retired. I believe his son runs the estates."

"Oh, I see," she said, not seeing at all. *Son?* Vikash hadn't mentioned anything about a son. So, Neelam had already been married and she'd have a stepson? The two boys in the photograph were too young to run a plantation. Perhaps the photo was an old one and they were now grown up. In which case, how old was Neelam?

"Anyway, mum's the word," the captain said tapping the side of his nose. "I do hope you don't think I've spoilt the surprise." He looked crestfallen.

"Oh no, Captain, not at all. You've been marvellous." She beamed at him, and he turned and walked briskly away, her heart thudding.

Her husband-to-be was retired? And she'd have a stepson?

She needed to speak to Vikash with all haste.

"Well, he's probably been married before, in fact, I think I remember Uncle saying something about him being a widower." Vikash twisted the ruby ring around his finger. "Does the thought of having a stepson bother you?"

"Vik! You've missed the point. Look at him. Does he look old enough to be retired and have a son who can run his business? He can't be more than thirty." Her brows drew together as something occurred to her. "How old is this photograph?"

Vikash shrugged.

Icy drops of dread trickled down her spine. This photo could be years old. Neelam could be twice her age. Did he look more like his father now? Her gaze slid to the grey-haired man. The freezing trickles of fear turned to a deluge.

No! It couldn't be ...

She'd only assumed the handsome, young man was Neelam. Perhaps he wasn't. Had her uncle arranged to marry her to the man she'd assumed was Neelam's father?

It was out of the question. Uncle Rahul wouldn't marry her off to that old man. But as she turned to Vikash to find the confirmation she sought, bile rose to the back of her throat, cutting off her words.

She recognised when Vikash was feeling guilty. The pink tips to his ears. His inability to meet her gaze and his need to fidget. Years ago, he used to turn a toy over and over in his hand, studiously watching it. Now, he twisted the ring around his finger.

*He knew?* Her own brother knew their uncle planned to marry her to a man who was older than Pop?

She moistened her lips and forced the words out. "Which one is Neelam Banerjee?"

"Well ..."

She waited, wanting to give him a chance to prove he hadn't known. But he couldn't look at her, much less the photograph.

She was finding it hard to breathe. "Y ... you knew, didn't you? You let me believe it was the young man and that I'd have a choice about marrying!"

"Samira! Be reasonable." His voice was petulant and demanding.

"I'm not going through with this! I will not marry a man older than our own grandfather." She stood up.

"Where are you going?" His eyes were wide in alarm, and he placed a restraining hand on her arm.

She shook him off. "I'm going to tell Uncle Rahul I have no intention of marrying that man or anyone else of his choice."

"No, wait!" Vikash grabbed her arm again. This time, he gripped her tightly.

"There are things you should know ... Uncle Rahul is used to getting his own way. He'll be furious."

"*I'm* furious! And I can't believe you're siding with him. When we get home, Papa will also be furious."

Vikash lowered his gaze and released his grip on her arm.

Tariq was waiting outside her room.

"I'm going to see Uncle Rahul." It was ridiculous she had to explain herself to this man.

"He is too busy to see you this morning."

"Then when can I see him?"

John appeared around the corner with a trolley on which was her breakfast.

"Morning, miss."

Tariq stepped forward to take the trolley from him, but he ignored the servant and pushed it into Samira's cabin.

"The scrambled eggs are quite delicious today, miss. I'd have brought you fresh towels first, but I thought you'd want the eggs before they get cold." He gave her a meaningful look, and as he removed the silver dome, he nudged the plate.

"Thank you, John," she said, looking at Tariq to make sure he didn't suspect anything. "I'm sure I'm going to enjoy them."

"I'll be back shortly to pick the tray up." He glanced at the writing pad on her desk and then back at the plate. "Just let me know if there's anything you need."

He closed the door firmly as he left.

Samira drew the bolt on the door and lifted the plate. There neatly folded, was an envelope containing two telegrams.

As she read them both, tears filled her eyes and trickled down her cheeks. They were both from Lexie. The first told her that Papa was well and had not sent a message asking her to come home. Furthermore, he advised her not to return to India because he'd discovered Uncle Rahul was going to force her to marry, with or without her consent. He was waiting to hear whether he should travel to England or to Bombay to be there when the ship docked.

The second telegram said Lexie and Archie would meet Samira when the *Aurora Crown* docked in Marseille and would take her home.

But if she disembarked in France, Uncle would insist Tariq accompanied her, so how would she get away?

Her mind whirled. Uncle Rahul and Vikash might truly believe they were acting in her best interests. Papa had been unwell in the past, so perhaps her brother had persuaded her to go home because he believed that was the best course of action. And it was she who'd jumped to conclusions about the photograph of the prospective bridegroom. Uncle hadn't forced her to do anything yet – other than to stop wearing the clothes she'd brought with her. But it was hardly a crime to lavish silks and satins, and expensive jewels on your niece. She hadn't been kept a prisoner in her cabin, even though Tariq had shadowed her everywhere. But both Uncle and Vikash had assured her it was for her safety. It had certainly put people off talking to her, but was that her uncle or her brother's fault?

If she confronted Uncle Rahul now and told him she wouldn't marry, would he merely deny he'd arranged a wedding and honeymoon? Simply claim Captain Rigby had made a mistake? It was like fighting shadows.

What could he do to her? That chilly feeling of doubt permeated her again. He'd already separated her from the other passengers, ensuring she was completely alone, other than her brother. And today, Vikash had shown where his loyalties lay.

Suppose Uncle Rahul wouldn't let her off the ship to meet Lexie and Archie in Marseille?

Seasickness had prevented her from leaving the ship when it had docked at Santander and Lisbon. When they'd stopped at Gibraltar, Uncle Rahul had strongly suggested she didn't go ashore, telling her there was absolutely nothing to see, and the torrential rain that had lashed the ship when it arrived in port persuaded her to remain onboard. Walking around in the rain with Tariq at her shoulder, hadn't been appealing. But that night as she'd sat at Uncle's table in the dining room, she'd overheard people talking about the Rock of Gibraltar and the Barbary Apes they'd seen that day, and wished she'd insisted on going ashore.

At the time, she'd assumed that coming from India, with its breath-taking scenery and wildlife, Uncle hadn't been impressed by a rocky promontory and a few monkeys, but now, she wondered if he'd simply wanted to ensure she didn't communicate with Papa or anyone else – the plan to marry her into the Banerjee family was more likely to be achieved if she were completely isolated and helpless.

A little later, however, when Uncle Rahul knocked at her door, she knew with certainty he wasn't acting in her best interests.

"Ah, my dear, I'm afraid I have some bad news for you ... Nothing for you to worry about I'm taking care of everything. Regrettably, there's an outbreak of a dreadful stomach virus on board. It's quite an epidemic. So, it would be best if you stayed in your cabin and didn't come to the dining room or mix with any of the passengers until it's run its course. Tariq will be on hand if you need anything and when he's resting, your brother will check on you. I've paid two stewards to prepare your food away from everyone else's and they alone will bring it to your cabin. Of course, as soon as there is no danger of being infected, you'll be free to wander about the ship again." He smiled, briefly nodded his head, and turning, he walked down the corridor towards his cabin. Tariq closed her door and turned the key.

So, she truly was a prisoner, without friends. Even her stewards were in the pay of her uncle.

At mid-morning, John appeared with his trolley laden with clean laundry.

"Miss," he said curtly without his usual smile. Tariq stood at the door with arms crossed, watching as John silently changed the sheets and remade the bed, before taking a pile of towels into the bathroom.

"Ted'll be here with your lunch," he said when he'd finished tidying her room. He pushed the trolley out of the cabin and left without looking at her. When he'd gone, Tariq closed the door and turned the key in the lock. Samira banged on the communicating door between her room and Vikash's but if her brother was in, he didn't reply.

She stood at the window for a while, staring out at the uninspiring horizon. It was as if an artist had painted a plain blue sky without birds or clouds over an expanse of sea on which nothing bobbed or sailed. The enormity and emptiness of the view echoed the feelings in her heart. How was she going to endure this solitude until they arrived in India? All thoughts of meeting Lexie in Marseille were now completely quashed. She wandered into the bathroom to wash the tears from her face and to brush her hair when she noticed the large pile of towels on the marble top. John usually placed them on the towel rails unless he'd left her a message, in which case, he placed them in a stack on the marble top. She lifted the top towel, hardly daring to believe she'd find anything after John's earlier unfriendliness, but there, beneath the top towel, was an envelope. With a glance over her shoulder, she seized it and tore it open to find several banknotes and a letter from John. He explained the money was from her Uncle who'd pressed it on him and Ted. They hadn't wanted to keep it since they had no intention of carrying out his orders and when Samira got off at Marseille, she'd need some money. She was to hide it until they could get her off the ship. He went on to say he'd informed the chief steward who was aware Samira was now practically a prisoner and he, in turn, had notified the captain, who'd been rather sceptical. Captain Rigby hadn't wanted to upset an important passenger such as Uncle Rahul, so it was unlikely any help would come from that quarter. But if the captain was not convinced her uncle was doing something unethical, he, Ted and the chief steward were, and they'd do everything they could to get her off the ship to meet her friends. He finished by assuring her there was no outbreak of sickness on the ship and that she shouldn't worry about anything.

For the first time since she'd boarded at Southampton, Samira felt there was certainty in her life and the lies and half-truths which had made up her world had been exposed. Nevertheless, the chances of meeting Lexie were slim, especially now the captain knew about Uncle Rahul's scheme – and still supported him.

Despite docking in Marseille, Samira's view from the cabin window hadn't changed – just sea and sky, although now birds were wheeling above, and boats sliced through the water. Would the ship leave as it had arrived, without Samira setting eyes on the shore, much less stepping on it?

John had delivered a note hidden under her dinner plate the previous evening, instructing her to be ready to leave in the morning. She'd been up since before dawn and had paced the cabin until John arrived with her breakfast. Tariq let him in and watched while he pushed the trolley towards the table ignoring Samira, then with a curt "Miss." He left.

To her enormous disappointment, there was no note hidden under her breakfast plate. She ate a small piece of roll and drank some lemon tea, but her stomach was so knotted with fear, she couldn't manage anything else. With eyes downcast, John collected the breakfast things from her room and after Tariq had locked her door, she heard the china clattering as he wheeled the trolley away down the corridor. Catching sight of herself in the dressing table mirror, she saw a young woman dressed in bright baggy, satin trousers, long silky tunic and a scarf. How on earth did she expect to slip away unnoticed dressed like that? She'd chosen the darkest *shalwar* and *kameez* in her wardrobe but even so, she would be more obvious dressed in those clothes, than the POWs on Joanna and Ben's farm who had large red dots sewn onto their overalls. She looked down at her jewel-encrusted sandals. How would she be able to run in those?

It was hopeless. She sank onto the stool and stared at her reflection. Her eyes were sunken and shadowed with purple smudges beneath. Luke had once said she had exotic eyes. Now, they were simply sad, resigned eyes.

# Chapter Eighteen

B y his own admission, Frank West wasn't very good at plumbing. Years ago, he'd been apprenticed to a plumber, but by mutual agreement, he'd left and taken up carpentry. After serving his apprenticeship, he'd got a job on the *Aurora Crown* and he had an excellent reputation. But apparently today, his skills with wood were not required.

"You don't have to do anything, just bash a few pipes and make it look like you're doing something." John handed Frank a large wooden toolbox of plumber's tools.

"You're barmy! Why don't you do it?"

"Because the servant knows us and it's going to look a bit suspicious if we suddenly turn up and pretend to fix the plumbing."

"But why me?"

"Because you're a good bloke and me an' Ted trust you. We'll both be there too but we need help. There's a couple of quid in it, courtesy of her uncle ..." John added.

"You're on."

Everyone knew about the beautiful, dark-skinned girl with the silent, brooding servant. No one except John and Ted had seen her for days. Her uncle had told the captain she was ill although when he'd offered to send the ship's doctor, the uncle had declined, saying he was sure she'd be well soon. The captain had confessed to the officers he was reluctant to get involved in a family squabble and risk upsetting such a rich passenger. It hadn't taken long for the story to spread to every member of the crew, on every part of the ship.

And now, Frank had been recruited to help rescue the girl – by tinkering with the plumbing. More specifically, his job was to ensure the girl's brother was out of his cabin for as long as it took to smuggle someone aboard and then to get them both off the ship.

He knocked on Vikash's door, holding his box of tools in front of him to lend credence to his story.

"Good morning, Mr Stewart, I'm sorry to bother you but I need to carry out some emergency repairs in your bathroom. I'm afraid the soil pipe's in danger of leaking and I need to deal with it now. I apologise for any inconvenience ..."

"Come in," said Vikash scarcely looking at the plumber and his tools. He returned to the desk and sat down.

Frank hesitated. He'd been instructed to make sure the cabin was empty, but Vikash had a large pile of papers in front of him and it looked like he'd be there for some time.

Going into the bathroom, Frank turned on all the taps and repeatedly banged the pipes under the sink with his wrench as hard as he dared without actually causing any damage. He'd been instructed to flood the bathroom, if necessary, as long as he got the man out of his bedroom.

Vikash appeared at the door. "How long are you going to keep making so much noise?" he asked crossly.

Frank smiled innocently. "I've only done a few preliminary tests so far, but it's going to get a lot noisier I'm afraid. And, of course, with a soil pipe, there could, of course, be … unpleasant … er … smells. Yeah, very unpleasant."

Vikash rolled his eyes in annoyance. "In that case, I'm going out. Ensure someone informs me when I can come back. And please hurry."

"Yes, of course, sir." Frank dared not breathe until Vikash had left, then he opened the door and furtively looked down the corridor to check Tariq was still in position outside Miss Stewart's cabin.

He knocked gently on the communicating door and waited.

Nothing.

He tapped again.

What on earth was going on? John had told him the young woman would be ready.

Eventually, she opened the door. If Frank had experienced any misgivings about this plumbing assignment, he lost them when he saw how wretched she appeared, and then how her face lit up with relief when she realised he was part of a rescue plan.

"Bring everything you need," he whispered.

She went back into the cabin and returned with a jewellery box and a toiletry bag.

"Is that all you're taking?"

She nodded. "There's nothing else of mine here."

Frank allowed her into Vikash's cabin, closed the communicating door softly and locked it.

"Thank you so much," she said, her eyes full of gratitude. "What do we do now?"

"I'll unlock the door and we wait for Ted to come."

Seconds later the steward entered the cabin with his trolley of fresh linen and locked the door behind him. He took Samira's suitcase out from under piles of sheets.

"You might be needing this, Miss Stewart," he said. "There appears to have been a mix-up and your suitcase accidentally ended up in your uncle's cabin." He winked.

"Oh, thank you." Samira opened the case and put her jewellery box and toiletry bag inside."

"So far, so good," said Frank. "Now what?"

"I'm going to take the trolley outside and I'll pretend to sort out the sheets. It'll block the big bloke's view of this end of the corridor and with any luck, John'll be along in a second or two to cause a distraction. When I signal, you come out and add to the confusion," he said to Frank. "Bring your toolbox."

Ted whistled tunelessly as he wheeled the trolley back out into the corridor, leaving the cabin door slightly ajar.

The rattle of china heralded John's approach and there was suddenly a crash, an enraged yell and the smash of plates. Ted's hand appeared around the door beckoning, and when Frank rushed into the corridor with his toolbox, he saw Tariq on the floor covered in food scraps and broken plates. Frank rushed forward and ensuring he was standing on Tariq's robes, he pretended to help him up.

Apologising repeatedly, John pretended to lift the trolley upright. After a few attempts, he'd manoeuvred it, so it completely blocked the corridor.

Tariq shoved Frank, sending him spinning down the corridor. Now his robes were free, the servant sprang to his feet, his sandals crunching on the broken crockery. Reaching inside his robes, he withdrew a dagger and lunged at John who leapt backwards narrowly missing the blade.

"Watch out, Frank! He's got a knife!"

Tariq swung around; his blade raised. With lightning speed, Frank rushed at the servant, slamming the wooden toolbox against the side of his head. With a grunt, Tariq sank to the floor.

Desperation lent the two stewards strength and they dragged the huge unconscious body into Samira's room and locked the door. John swept up the broken pieces of china and food remnants, while Frank picked up all the tools that had fallen out of his box.

"Got his knife?" John asked.

Frank nodded. There'd be trouble when the big bloke came round but if they could show he'd threatened them with a knife, they'd be in the clear.

Several minutes later, Ted came out of Vikash Stewart's cabin and give the thumbs-up signal. Two women in floral summer dresses slipped out of the cabin and followed Ted away, along the corridor. The women walked swiftly, arm in arm. The one with bubbly blonde hair that bounced as she walked, was holding Miss Stewart's suitcase. The other was wearing a large summer hat which she held on tightly and which completely hid her hair. She turned briefly before turning the corner and waved.

# Chapter Nineteen

♥

Samira and Lexie found Archie pacing back and forth along the deck while he waited to escort them off the *Aurora Crown*. When he saw them, he enveloped Samira in a huge hug, kissed Lexie briefly on the cheek and took the suitcase.

"My brave girl," he said proudly and steered them down the gangplank.

As they reached the shore, Samira turned to check Uncle Rahul or Vikash weren't following. There was no sign of them, but she was thrilled to see three members of the crew – John, Ted and Frank – leaning over the rails, waving madly. She blew them a kiss and waved back.

A cab was waiting for them, and Archie helped the girls into the back with the suitcase, then climbing in the front, he gave instructions to the driver in perfect French.

Lexie and Samira clung together as the car wove through the crowds around the fish market and sped through the narrow streets of Marseille.

"Darling, I thought we'd never see you again." Lexie stroked Samira's hair.

Samira was beyond words, she simply sobbed.

"You're going home, Samira, don't worry, darling. Please don't cry. Archie and I won't let anything happen to you."

Finally, Samira felt safe enough to tell Lexie and Archie about her uncle's plans to marry her off. "I can't believe my own brother didn't warn me. How could he have gone along with it?"

"Don't be too hard on him, darling, your father and I have been sending each other lots of telegrams. He's found out Vikash ran up some gambling debts which your uncle paid. Your father thinks your uncle is taking repayment in the form of cooperation. Once your father pays the debt, Vikash won't be under any obligation. After that, either he shows loyalty towards his father and sister or ... Well, I suppose he doesn't."

Archie turned around. "It might be an idea to tell Samira now, Lexie." The tone of his voice suggested she might not welcome the news.

"Er, yes, I suppose so." Lexie paused and swallowed. "Now, darling, I don't want you to panic ... and I know this isn't going to be quite what you wanted but ... In order to get here, we didn't have any choice ... and it's all going to be right ... it's just that ..."

"Lexie, you're frightening me. Please just tell me."

"Right, yes of course. It's just that ... well, Archie and I are going to get married—"

"But that's wonderful, Lexie! Congratulations! Why on earth did you think I'd panic? I'm so pleased for you ..." She paused. "Oh Lexie, if you mean because it didn't work out between Luke and me, and you thought it would remind me, there's no need. That's the first piece of good news I've had for some time."

"Er, well, no. That's not it exactly. It's just that we'll be getting married soon and after, we're going to live in France. Archie's thinking of joining an aeronautical engineering company in Toulouse – and that's where we're going now. That means you'll be going back to England alone. I'm so sorry but there wouldn't be room for all of us anyway ..."

"There wouldn't be room? Where?"

"Yes," Lexie said slowly. "That's the part you're not going to like. We flew down in Archie's plane. Now, I know you don't like the thought of flying but really, darling, it's not frightening at all."

The colour drained from Samira's face. "Fly? Lexie, I ... I'm not sure I ..." There must be another way. She couldn't go up in an aeroplane. Her heart was thrashing in her chest at the thought of being so high in the sky.

"It's the fastest way home, darling. Ben and Joanna will be waiting for you at the airfield, and they'll take you straight home and the whole terrible ordeal will be over. But it just needs a bit of courage ... And I'm afraid, there's no other way of getting you home safely."

Archie carried a limp Samira in his arms to the grey Beechcraft Staggerwing F17D waiting on the airfield, while Lexie followed with her suitcase.

"Are you sure she's all right?" Lexie asked. "I thought those tablets you gave her were supposed to calm her down, not knock her out." She took small skips to keep up with long-legged Archie, who was striding across the grass even with Samira in his arms.

"Don't fuss, darling, she's still breathing, and it might be a blessing in disguise. My mother lives on those tablets, so they can't be that strong," he said over his shoulder.

"Perhaps you should have only given her one. And I'm not sure the brandy helped. I don't think you're supposed to mix medicine and alcohol."

"I didn't have much choice, darling, she couldn't swallow them and by the look on her face, I thought she was about to be sick. At least the brandy eased them down."

"Yes, I suppose so. And she's not trembling anymore. D'you think she'll sleep the whole way home?"

"I wouldn't have thought so. But then I didn't expect her to be like this. Lyon Bron Aerodrome's about an hour away, and she'll have to get out while they refuel. I just hope she'll be sleepy enough to get back in the plane for the second leg of the journey. Then it's about two and a half hours to Essex. But I'm not sure what'll happen if she refuses to get back on board at Lyon."

"Well, at least she's out of the clutches of her uncle. I suppose we'll just have to worry about that if it happens. What a shame she's so afraid of flying. This all could have worked out so differently. It could have been such an opportunity ..." Lexie sighed.

"Darling, you're incorrigible."

"I know but I can't give up hope. We're so happy, Archie, I just wish Samira could be. I'm sure if they just talked things over ..."

Archie managed to manoeuvre the sleeping girl through the small door with the help of the pilot, and strapping her into the seat, he placed her headset on. Then handing the suitcase to the pilot, he shook his hand, slapped him on the shoulder and jumped down from the plane's lower wing.

Lexie blew the pilot a kiss. "Look after her Luke, or you'll have me to answer to," she shouted up at the cockpit.

If only they'd let her lie down and sleep. Samira had tried to fight the tiredness, but she was so weak, she barely had the strength to open her eyelids, let alone raise her head off her chest. Every so often, she managed to prise her eyes open a fraction and peer out through narrow slits, but her lids were so heavy, they immediately dropped. What she saw when her eyes opened made no sense. Blurry shapes. Shadows. Hazy hints of something, then nothing.

She longed to lie down but straps held her upright in a confined space. Was she in a car? It was the only thing that made sense and yet the rumble not only filled her ears but also vibrated throughout her body. And a smell – something like petrol filled her nostrils.

No, it couldn't be a car. And yet ... how else could she be moving at speed over uneven ground? Her head bobbed up and down. Such a bumpy ride. Like driving a tractor over a rutted field.

Faster. Faster. The rumble swelled to a roar and her head bobbed harder and wilder.

Open your eyes.

She *would* open them. She'd open her eyes and look. But it was no good, they simply weren't responding, and her eyelids remained closed.

A teeth-jarring jolt and thankfully, the bumping stopped. And yet she wasn't stationary. The sensation of moving forward persisted although now, she was tilted backwards, her weight pushed towards the back of the chair – it was as if the car had simply lifted off the ground and was facing up to the sky.

It was too difficult to understand. She'd sleep a while. When she woke, she'd have more energy, and everything would become clear. Yes, the more she thought about it, sleep seemed to be the best option.

Minutes later? Hours? A stab of pain as Samira's ears popped, dragging her back to consciousness. Something was different. The ever-present hum had changed tempo. She was leaning forward, held in place with straps. Then, a shuddering thud.

She gasped and for a second, the shock jolted her into semi-wake-fulness. Through half-opened eyes, she saw a blur of countryside moving past her at speed. As the noise increased, the car came to a standstill.

Peace at last. Her chin dropped to her chest. Sleep.

But no. It wasn't to be. A warm breeze displaced the stuffy air in the car and hands pulled at the straps that restricted her. If she'd had the strength, she'd have pushed the hands away. But even after her sleep, she hadn't regained her strength.

Something was wrong. This wasn't normal. Why couldn't she wake up?

And then the nightmare began.

Uncle Rahul was there. He lifted her out of the car. Around him, men spoke in a foreign language. Then, he passed her to someone else. Tariq? She was being carried in someone's arms. So, Uncle Rahul had found her. The escape attempt had failed.

She tried to scream, but her voice didn't respond. What was the point anyway? Who'd come if she called? If Uncle Rahul was here with his servants speaking in a different language, she must be in India.

There was no escape. Uncle Rahul had won and when she finally awoke, she'd have to do as he wanted. Her head flopped against his shoulder in submission. Strangely, her cheek lay against leather. And rather than the sweet, sickly smell of patchouli oil which often accompanied her uncle and his servant, she could smell something spicy. Luke. The scent reminded her of Luke.

Relief flooded through her. It was a dream. Soon she'd awaken. But in the meantime, this was now like so many of the images that had filled her nights: being in Luke's arms. Holding tightly around his neck as he carried her in the woods near their well. Her senses filled with him. She sank deeper into the dream while Luke carried her into the darkness.

She woke up in the bedroom she'd shared with Lexie in Priory Hall. Joanna sat next to her bed, and she smiled when Samira opened her eyes.

"Hello, sleepy. You've given us quite a turn. How are you feeling now?"

Samira groaned as she moved. Pain flooded her head.

"Better." The sound was no more than a croak, her mouth was so dry.

Joanna helped her to sit up and held a glass of water to her lips.

"Just sips, Samira. A little at a time." She paused. "You have Lexie and Archie to blame for this, you know. Fancy giving you medicine which hadn't been prescribed for you. And with alcohol too. I spoke to Lexie on the telephone and gave her a piece of my mind. It's no wonder the tablets affected you so badly. She said you'd told her you hadn't eaten much and hadn't been sleeping, so that wouldn't have helped."

"Don't be cross," Samira whispered. "They rescued me. And Lexie was very brave, coming on to the ship to get me."

"Yes, I suppose so. Now, tell me ..." Joanna's tone changed completely. "What do you remember of the flight home?"

"Flight?"

Joanna nibbled her bottom lip. "Ah, I see you don't remember much then."

"You mean I was on an aero*plane*?" Samira tried to sit up and groaned again.

"Yes, it's Archie's. He bought it a few weeks ago. We thought it would be the fastest way to get you home. Can you remember anything at all about the journey?"

Samira sank back into the pillows. "No. It was all like a dream. Just a blur. I thought I was in a car but everything's starting to make sense.

Now I recall Lexie saying something about flying home, but I can't remember much after that. It's probably just as well I was asleep."

"So, you don't remember being carried off the plane at Lyon or back on after refuelling?"

"No. I had lots of disturbing dreams. At one point, I thought my uncle was taking me away."

"And ... er ... do you remember the pilot?"

"No, not at all." She looked at Joanna's serious expression and suddenly, her heart leapt. "Was it Luke? Did he bring me home?"

Joanna nodded.

Excitement bubbled up inside. "Where is he?"

Joanna looked at Samira sadly. "I'm sorry, love, he's gone back to Devon. He slept here last night but he left first thing this morning."

Samira sank back on the pillows. Luke hadn't bothered to say goodbye. He hadn't even waited until she'd woken up to see she was all right. So, Archie had asked for a favour and once Luke had completed his task, he'd gone home.

He truly had moved on.

Well, now she must do the same.

Faye brought Samira a plate of toast and after she'd eaten, insisted on brushing her hair.

"I'll pin it up for you if you like," Faye said.

"No, darling, that's fine thank you. Now, why don't you tell me what you've been up to while I've been away?"

"Oh, you know, dreary school. Boring stuff. I'd rather hear about you. Mama said your uncle tried to marry you to someone you'd never met. Was he a prince?"

"No, I don't think so. But it wouldn't have mattered what he was. I didn't want to marry him."

"He might have been very handsome like a prince."

"He wasn't very handsome at all. If you'd like to see, I still have a photograph of him. It's in my suitcase."

Faye fetched the photograph. "He looks handsome to me."

"Yes, that man is very nice looking, but he wasn't the one my uncle wanted me to marry." She pointed at the old man. "It was this one."

"Oh no, Samira! He's so old. He's even older than Papa. Why did your uncle want you to marry him?"

"Things are different in India, darling. There are different customs. My uncle was trying to form a bond with a very rich family. It would have helped his business."

"Business? But people marry for love." Faye put her hands on her hips, her face displaying outrage.

Samira suppressed a smile. "Well, they do usually, but not always in India."

"But you're not Indian, Samira. This is your home. You belong here. I hope I never meet your uncle because I'd want to tell him off and if I did that, Mama would tell *me* off for using unladylike language, but I think sometimes, there's a need for it, don't you, Samira?"

"Faye!" It was Joanna at the bedroom door. "Let's give Samira a chance rest. I think her hair is fine now, love."

When Samira was alone, she thought about Faye's words 'But you're not Indian, Samira. This is your home. You belong here.'

Well, of course, she was Indian – well, half-Indian anyway. And her mother's heritage was very precious, but she had spent so many of her formative years in England she felt more comfortable here. It had taken a cruise with an unscrupulous uncle to show her where she really belonged – and a child to point it out to her. She felt slightly stronger having decided where her future lay.

Not only was Faye instrumental in showing Samira where she'd spend her future, the young girl also gave her an idea about how she would fill her time.

It came about a few days after Samira had arrived home. Faye was staring wistfully out of the kitchen window.

"What's the matter, darling?" Samira asked.

"I wanted to ride my pony, but I've got a spelling test at school tomorrow and I keep getting them wrong. I'll never learn them. Stupid spellings. What's the point of spellings? It's simply preposterous."

Samira turned away to hide her smile. 'Preposterous' was Faye's favourite word, and she currently used it as often as she could.

"Show me those preposterous spellings, darling, and we'll find a way for you to remember them. Then you'll be able to ride Rainbow. Let's get some paper."

Faye groaned. "It's no good, Samira, I keep writing the words down but as soon as I think I've learned them, I find I've forgotten them."

"We're not going to write them, darling, we're going to draw them."

Joanna came into the kitchen half an hour later to find them laughing at the stickmen and other drawings that Samira had drawn to illustrate the spellings.

"See, you won't forget the 'O' in 'people' because there's a face inside that 'O' and she's looking at you, telling you to remember," said Samira, giving the face in the letter 'O' curls on top of her head.

"Test me, test me, Mama! Samira and I've done lots of drawings and made funny pictures of all the words and now I think I can remember them."

"That's wonderful, love." Joanna gave Samira a grateful smile.

"I wish Samira was my teacher, she makes learning stuff so much fun. Not like grumpy, old Miss Stephens," said Faye.

Teaching. That was something Samira would like to do. Why not? Yes, she'd find out how to become a teacher.

That evening, something else happened that was to change the course of her life.

The doorbell rang and Samira answered it, to find Pop standing on the doorstep.

# Chapter Twenty

♥

M rs Thomsett's face lit up with a smile. "Oh, Samira! How lovely to see you, lovey. I can't believe you're back after so long. Well, what a wonderful way to welcome in the New Year! Come in, come in." She led the way down the hall to the kitchen, a toddler balanced on her right hip and a baby in the crook of her beefy arm. "What a shame you didn't come before, you could've spent Christmas with us. Still, it's so good to see you."

She waved her hand for two children to get off an armchair and indicated Samira should sit.

"My Sally's latest additions," Mrs Thomsett said, nodding at the children. "Remember she was in the family way when you left? She's got four now. But tell me all about you. Are you going to stay?"

"Yes, Pop's tenants have moved out and I'm going to live here. I'm going to study to be a teacher."

"Well, that's wonderful news, lovey. Just wait 'til I tell the neighbours. Those tenants never really fit in. Hoity-toity they were. Thought they were too good for Aylward Street. I'm glad to see the back o' them and doubly glad to have our bit of exotic back. My Wilf will be so chuffed to see you, lovey. He always said you was a nice girl

– and now look at you. Quite a young lady. And you're going to be a teacher. Bless me!"

Over the next few days, Samira cleaned Pop's house from top to bottom and in memory of Gran, she made sure there were vases of flowers in the windows. She cleaned the spare room and made it ready for the arrival of her guest at the weekend. Lexie's wedding would take place in four months' time on the first of May, and she'd asked Samira and Faye to be her bridesmaids. Mark was to be a page boy, much to his disgust.

"And Luke?" Samira had asked with dread. "I expect he's best man?"

Lexie had nodded. "Please say you'll come though, Samira. I'll be devastated if you don't, and it'll ruin Faye's day too. She's so looking forward to it."

Samira sighed; she would go. It would be unkind to refuse and anyway, she wanted to be at her best friend's wedding. She'd simply keep out of Luke's way. After all, they were both adults – they would be civil towards each other.

"Yes, Lexie, of course I'll be your bridesmaid. I'd be honoured."

"Darling!" Lexie threw her arms round Samira's neck and hugged her. "There's something else ..."

Samira guessed from Lexie's tone it was something she didn't want to hear.

"I'm really sorry, darling, but Luke may bring a ... er ... friend to the wedding. Mummy said he's been seeing a neighbour – a widow. She lost her husband during the war. She has two children, and they may come too."

It hadn't come as a complete surprise to Samira, but it still felt like something inside her had died.

Samira had put off cleaning the cast iron range. Pop's tenants hadn't looked after it and while she dealt with the rest of the house, she'd ignored it, but with Lexie arriving the next day, she decided it was time to do something about it. The two young women had planned to travel into the centre of London to look for fabric for the bride's and bridesmaids' dresses, and since Archie's parents had offered to pay for the whole event, apparently, money was no object. Lexie was looking forward to buying the material and lace which was now becoming available after the austerity they'd become accustomed to during the war.

Samira scrubbed at the baked-on food residue and wished she'd thought to tie her hair back before she'd started. She repeatedly wiped wisps off her face and tucked them behind her ears as she leant forward trying to clean the back of the oven.

There was a knock on the door, and she called "Come in."

When no one appeared, she called again, "Come in, the door's open." Still no one arrived, so with a sigh, she found a tea towel, wiped her hands and went to the front door. A glance in the hall mirror showed several dirty smudges on her cheeks where she'd pushed hair out of her eyes, and she rubbed at them with the cloth.

"It's open," she called, expecting to see one of Mrs Thomsett's grandchildren or great-grandchildren waiting.

There were indeed children outside her door, but they hadn't knocked – instead, some were admiring a motorbike which was parked at the kerb, and others were gaping at the man on her doorstep.

"Luke!" Samira gasped, her hands flying to her mouth.

"Stop gawpin' at Samira's guest," said Mrs Thomsett, who was there so rapidly, she must have been looking through her window and seen the stranger approach. The children made no attempt to move and neither did Mrs Thomsett who looked pointedly at Samira, and with theatrical extravagance, licked her finger and pretended to wipe her face.

"You'd better come in," said Samira, standing back to allow Luke into the hall. A glance in the mirror showed her what Mrs Thomsett had been trying to warn her – when she'd put her hand to her mouth she'd left behind black smears. She scrubbed them vigorously with the tea towel, leaving red marks. The next time she saw Luke, she'd imagined she'd look glamorous in her bridesmaid outfit, not dirty, with smudges on her face. How dare he just turn up unannounced like that and catch her at her worst. Anger bubbled inside her.

She followed him into the kitchen and motioned for him to sit, "Tea?" she asked, aware her question, sounded more like a challenge.

"No thank you, Samira."

Her stomach constricted as she looked into his eyes. How could they be bluer than she remembered? She wondered if it had been a way of protecting herself during the months after he'd gone – her memory had diluted the entire essence of him – the paler and more nebulous he became, the easier it was to cope with the loss.

She sat opposite him, perched on the edge of the chair, clutching the wooden arms, waiting for him to speak. "So?" she said finally.

He was having trouble finding the words. "Lexie asked me to talk to you," he began and then paused.

"Let me guess. She wants to make sure there won't be any awkward moments at her wedding. Well, there's no need to worry, I shall keep well away from you. I shall smile in photographs when we're put together, but other than that, you don't need to worry about me ..."

"No, it wasn't that, Samira. It wasn't that at all ..."

Her anger dissipated slightly as she saw his disquiet.

"Lexie told me to explain ... She said I owed it to you." He looked down at the floor.

"Ah, that," said Samira, "well, don't bother. It's all quite straightforward. You found you didn't love me, and you left. It seems simple to me."

He shook his head sadly, "No, it wasn't like that."

"Well, what was it like then?" she snapped. "One minute we were talking about our future together and the next, you'd gone. You didn't answer any of my letters ..."

He sighed and lowered his head. "I left you because I couldn't bear to ..."

"Oh, just say it, Luke. You don't want me. Be honest. I once thought you were the bravest person in the world, flying those terrifying machines, facing death each day. But now, I'm beginning to wonder."

Luke got to his feet; his face flushed. "All right, I'll tell you." He swallowed and looked away from her as if he couldn't bring himself to admit it. "I left you because I couldn't bear to see the pity on your face when you heard it was unlikely I'd ever father children."

Her brows drew together. What was he talking about? "I don't understand. What have children got to do with anything?"

He leant forward, elbows on his knees and looked down at his dangling hands. "After I had mumps, there were complications ... The doctors said I might not be able to father children ..."

Samira's eyes were wide with horror. "And that's it? You left me because you couldn't have children?" She shook her head, her voice rising with incredulity. "You didn't think to tell me? To ask if I minded? When people love each other, don't they deal with problems together?" She was shouting now, the hurt of him leaving her, driving her on.

"Well, it didn't take you long to find someone else, did it? Presumably your new lady knows about this and doesn't mind?" she asked bitterly.

"My new lady?"

"Lexie said you were seeing a neighbour ... Oh, no! Of course, it all makes sense now. She already has children."

"Cathy? Oh, no, Samira, no! Cathy's just a friend, nothing more. I trained with her husband, and I know she's struggling financially. I swear there's nothing going on with her. It's you I love. I always have, I always will."

He was looking at her now, his blue eyes fixed on her face – honest, pleading.

She stared at him.

All those months of pain.

All those unnecessary tears.

She sank back into her chair. Empty. Hollow. Numb.

"But you just left." Her voice was no more than a croak.

He knelt in front of her.

"When we talked about our future, we often mentioned the family we'd have when the war was over. I knew if I told you I couldn't father children you'd pity me, but you wouldn't break it off – you're too kind and caring. One day, I thought you'd resent me, perhaps even despise me. I couldn't bear that, and I couldn't bear to make you unhappy. I thought if I left, you'd find someone else and settle down. Ben's neighbour seemed very keen on you. He could have given you a good life. And probably children too."

"But I didn't want him. And I'm not even bothered about children. I only wanted you ..." the lump in her throat wouldn't allow her to finish speaking.

He drew her to him and held her while she sobbed.

Mrs Thomsett crept along Samira's hall and quietly let herself out into the street. When she'd heard raised voices, she'd wanted to make sure Samira was all right. You couldn't be too careful these days. Something had been troubling the young woman since she'd been home and now Mrs Thomsett knew it had been the handsome, blond man.

Men! They wanted a bloomin' good shaking, the lot of them. Why didn't they just talk things over like women did? The stupid idiot could have saved himself – and more importantly, Samira – a lot of heartache. The world was full of children. Most of them seemed to live full or part-time in her house.

Didn't he know about adopting?

Didn't he know about medical treatment?

Didn't he know Samira was one in a million?

"Stupid, bloomin' man!" she muttered as she went into her house and took up her position by the window. "If he upsets Samira again," she said wagging her finger at a group of toddlers playing on the floor. "I'll 'ave 'is guts for garters, you see if I don't!"

Samira placed a hand on Luke's arm. "You won't want to come shopping for fabric."

"I'm not letting you out of my sight and if that means I must follow you up and down Oxford Street, that's what I'll do. Lexie won't mind if I come with you both tomorrow. She's been on at me for weeks to come and see you. She'll be thrilled."

"So, does she know why you left me?"

"No, I haven't told anyone." He looked down as if ashamed. "I didn't want anyone to know. I didn't even go back for more medical tests." He placed a finger under her chin and tilted it up. "Do you want me to go for tests?" he asked, looking deeply into her eyes.

"If *you* want to. As far as I'm concerned, I've got you back and if children come along one day, I'll be happy and if not ... well, I'll be just as happy because I have you." She hugged him tightly.

"I can't believe I so nearly lost you. If it wouldn't upstage Lexie and Archie's wedding, I'd marry you now," said Luke.

"We could do the next best thing ..."

"Yes?"

"We could exchange vows in our temple. It wouldn't be legally binding, but we would know we belonged to each other until after Lexie's wedding, then we could have a quiet ceremony in a church."

"You mean ...?"

She nodded. "Yes, our place."

Early on Sunday morning, Samira climbed on to the back of Luke's bike and wrapped her arms tightly around his waist. The engine roared to life and Luke drove carefully along the cobbled road, turned into Jamaica Street, and headed towards Mile End Road. Samira remembered the last time Luke had driven her in Ben's car to Priory Hall and how nervous she'd been, believing he would think her naïve and foolish. She closed her eyes and allowed the wind to whip through her hair, blowing away the pain of the last few months, leaving room for optimism for the future.

The sun was still low in the sky when they reached One Tree Hill. Luke helped her dismount and pulled her to him, holding her face in his hands.

"Are you ready for this, Samira?"

"Yes." She smiled up at him.

He took her hand and led her into the woods. The last time they'd come, they'd been bathed in soft, green light as the sun's rays penetrated the thick canopy of leaves. Now, however, the trees were bare and there was a sprinkling of rime over the boughs. They sparkled and glittered in the muted sunlight. Covered in frost, the tiny domed temple glistened like a magical, fairy palace and with their breath hanging in the air, Luke enveloped Samira in his arms and kissed her tenderly.

"I'll love and treasure you for as long as you'll have me, Samira."

"Then you're mine forever," she said.

END

Dawn would be thrilled if you would consider leaving a review for this book on Amazon and Goodreads, thank you.

If you'd like to know more about her books, please check out her website: dawnknox.com Also, you can find a gift of various short stories and further information about Dawn's writing.

## About the Author

Dawn spent much of her childhood making up stories filled with romance, drama and excitement. She loved fairy tales, although if she cast herself as a character, she'd more likely have played the part of the Court Jester than the Princess. She didn't recognise it at the time, but she was searching for the emotional depth in the stories she read. It wasn't enough to be told the Prince loved the Princess, she wanted to know how he felt and to see him declare his love. She wanted to see the wedding. And so, she'd furnish her stories with those details.

Nowadays, she hopes to write books that will engage readers' passions. From poignant stories set during the First World War to the zany antics of the inhabitants of the fictitious town of Basilwade; and from historical romances to the fantasy adventures of a group of anthropomorphic animals led by a chicken with delusions of grandeur, she explores the richness and depth of human emotion.

A book by Dawn will offer laughter or tears – or anything in between, but if she touches your soul, she'll consider her job well done.

If you'd like to keep in touch, please look for her newsletter on her blog and receive a welcome gift, containing an exclusive prequel to **The Duchess of Sydney,** several short, humorous stories, her inspiration in Plotlands and two photo-stories from **The Great War.** Periodically, she adds stories to it.

Following Dawn:

Blog: dawnknox.com

Amazon Author Central: https://mybook.to/DawnKnox

X: https://twitter.com/SunriseCalls

Instagram: https://www.instagram.com/sunrisecalls/

YouTube: https://tinyurl.com/mtcpdyms

# Also by Dawn Knox

**A Cottage in Plotlands**

The Heart of Plotlands Saga – Book One

London's East End to the Essex countryside - will a Plotlands cottage bring Joanna happiness or heartache?

1930 – Eighteen-year-old Joanna Marshall arrives in Dunton Plotlands friendless and alone. When her dream to live independently is cruelly shattered, her neighbours step in. Plotlanders look after their own. But they can't help Joanna when she falls in love with Ben Richardson – a man who is her social superior... and her boss.

Can Joanna and Ben find a place where rigid social rules will allow them to love?

Order from Amazon: https://mybook.to/ACottageInPlotlands

Paperback: ISBN: 9798378843756   eBook: ASIN: B0C4Y9VZY9

Also, **A Canary Girl in Plotlands, A Reunion in Plotlands** and **A Rose in Plotlands**

## The Duchess of Sydney

The Lady Amelia Saga – Book One

Betrayed by her family and convicted of a crime she did not commit, Georgiana is sent halfway around the world to the penal colony of Sydney, New South Wales. Aboard the transport ship, the Lady Amelia, Lieutenant Francis Brooks, the ship's agent becomes her protector, taking her as his "sea-wife" – not because he has any interest in her but because he has been tasked with the duty.

Despite their mutual distrust, the attraction between them grows. But life has not played fair with Georgiana. She is bound by family secrets and lies. Will she ever be free again – free to be herself and free to love?

Order from Amazon:  mybook.to/TheDuchessOfSydney

Paperback: ISBN: 9798814373588   eBook: ASIN: B09Z8LN4G9

Audiobook: ASIN: B0C86LG3Y4

Also, **The Finding of Eden,**
**The Other Place,**
**The Dolphin's Kiss,**
**The Pearl of Aphrodite**
and
**The Wooden Tokens**

Printed in Great Britain
by Amazon

47346339R00126